McQUAID'S GUN

McQUAID'S GUN

Wayne C. Lee

GUNSMOKE

First published in the UK by Isis

This hardback edition 2012
by AudioGO Ltd
by arrangement with
Golden West Literary Agency

ISBN 978 1 445 82415 4

British Library Cataloguing in Publication Data available.

Printed and bound in Great Britain by
MPG Books Group Limited

Wayne C. Lee was born to pioneering homesteaders near Lamar, Nebraska. His parents were old when he was born and it was an unwritten law since the days of the frontier that it was expected that the youngest child would care for the parents in old age. Having grown up reading novels by Zane Grey and William MacLeod Raine, Lee wanted to write Western stories himself. His best teachers were his parents. They might not be able to remember what happened last week by the time Lee had reached his majority, but they shared with him their very clear memories of the pioneer days. In fact they talked so much about that period that it sometimes seemed to Lee he had lived through it himself. Lee wrote a short story and let his mother read it. She encouraged him to submit it to a magazine and said she would pay the postage. It was accepted and appeared as *Death Waits at Paradise Pass* in *Lariat Story Magazine.* In the many Western novels that he has written since, violence has never been his primary focus, no matter what title a publisher might give one of his stories, but rather the interrelationships between the characters and within their communities. These are the dominant characteristics in all of Lee's Western fiction and create the ambiance so memorable in such diverse narratives as *The Gun Tamer* (1963), *Petticoat Wagon Train* (1972), and *Arikaree War Cry* (1992). In the truest sense Wayne C. Lee's Western fiction is an outgrowth of his impulse to create imaginary social fabrics on the frontier and his stories are intended primarily to entertain a reader at the same time as to articulate what it was about these pioneering men and women that makes them so unique and intriguing to later generations. His pacing, graceful style, natural sense of humor, and the genuine liking he feels toward the majority of his characters, combined with a commitment to the reality and power of romance between men and women as a decisive factor in making it possible for them to have a better life together than they could ever hope to have apart, are what most distinguish his contributions to the Western story.

I

Dan McQuaid rode into Long Bow Valley with the greatest of caution. For a man whose name struck fear into the hearts of supposedly brave men, McQuaid exercised great wariness of anything he didn't fully understand. And he didn't understand the situation in Long Bow Valley.

He had stopped at the courthouse at Pinedale to be sure that Cliff Usta could give him legal title, clear of all entanglements, to the land he had promised him. He discovered that Cliff Usta did not even own the land he had offered as wages for the use of McQuaid's gun in the battle shaping up in Long Bow Valley.

That had verified McQuaid's suspicions. There was something terribly wrong when a man offered as payment a piece of land that he didn't even own. Maybe it was something wrong with the man. Maybe it was something wrong with the whole setup. McQuaid's instincts told him to turn around and ride away from this while he still could.

But he wanted that land. He'd been here once on a hunting trip. He'd seen the land on Hatchet Creek that Cliff Usta had offered. It was worth fighting a war over. But if Usta didn't own it, he couldn't deed it over to McQuaid. Usta very likely hadn't expected McQuaid to find that out. At least, not until after the battle.

When McQuaid learned at the courthouse in Pinedale

that the land had been claimed by John Harris illegally for years and had been declared free land only when Harris's estate was settled, he decided on the spur of the moment to file papers on it himself. Now what would happen when Cliff Usta and his brother-in-law, Frank Patzel, found out he was to be the legal owner of the land?

He rode slowly along the road leading to Arrow, the only town in the valley. This was the best ranch country McQuaid had ever seen. Not only could the best cattle be raised here but also some of the best hay in the Rockies. There was a hungry market for the beef in the mining camps and there was always a market for hay.

McQuaid reached the town and rode cautiously up the street. Arrow was perched on the west bank of Long Bow Creek, which tumbled along in a southeast direction. It wasn't much of a town, but there wasn't much of a reason for a town being here, so it fit the needs very adequately.

McQuaid reined in at the one general store. Dismounting, he stepped up on the porch and looked over the town before going inside. A saddle shop and a hardware store along with a barbershop joined the general store on one side of the street.

Across from the general store was a big building. The door was closed so McQuaid couldn't see inside. But he guessed it was the meeting place of Arrow. Likely church was held there on Sunday, school on week days, and probably dances on Saturday nights.

A smaller building next to it advertised billiards. Likely a man could wet his whistle there and play cards, as well as shoot pool.

McQuaid sighed. He'd seen many towns like this, most of them down on the plains in ranching country. But this was ranching country, too, not mining country, and the town catered to the people who made it.

The inside of the store seemed dark to McQuaid after

coming in from the bright midday sunlight. There seemed to be only a man and a woman there, and both were behind counters. There were no other customers and that was the way McQuaid liked it. Maybe these two would tell him some of the things he had to know before he rode up the valley.

McQuaid bought some things he'd need to eat in the next few days. The man was all smiles as McQuaid ran up what must have seemed to him like a nice order.

"Good ranch country," McQuaid said as he paid his bill.

"The best," the man said. "More fighting than ranching going on now, though."

"You don't get rich fighting," McQuaid said.

"Tell that to John Harris's two stubborn daughters." The storekeeper squinted at McQuaid. "You ain't figuring on staying in Long Bow Valley, are you?"

"Might. Any reason why I shouldn't?"

"Could be—unless you like to fight."

"Not particularly fond of it," McQuaid said. "Who's this Harris and his two daughters?"

"John Harris came in here long ago. Took over this whole valley. Owned it all or at least kept everybody else out. Had two girls. Just as stubborn, bullheaded, and greedy as John himself. They married a couple of John's cowhands. Had families of their own. Everything was fine till Old John died a while back. His will divided the ranch between the girls. But each girl thinks she and her man ought to have it all."

McQuaid nodded. "Family fight. I always swore I'd stay out of family fights and church fights."

"You stay here, you'll have to do some fancy stepping to keep out of this family fight."

"Is it a shooting war or just words?"

"Ain't nobody been killed yet," the storekeeper said. "But it ain't far from it. Cliff Usta has the home buildings.

He also has John Harris's brand, the Long Bow. Since he married the oldest girl, he thinks he ought to have the whole valley."

"The other daughter has the other half of the valley," the woman put in, apparently not content any longer to let her husband tell the whole story. "She married a cowboy named Frank Patzel. They've got their headquarters on this side of the creek. Use the Hatchet brand. She is just as dead set as her sister on running the whole valley."

"Where do you stand in this?"

"Right in the middle, holding our breath," the man said. "They both buy from us and so far neither one has accused us of siding with the other one."

"They can't afford to make you their enemy," Mc-Quaid guessed. "Where else would they get what they have to buy?"

"Pinedale, I reckon," the man said. "But that's a long haul."

"You don't favor one side over the other?"

"Mister, even if I did, I sure wouldn't tell anybody," the man said.

McQuaid nodded. "You'll get along all right. Straddling a fence is something like riding a bony horse bareback. It ain't very comfortable, but it'll get you there if you don't fall off."

"If you're looking for a job, I'd advise you to try somewhere else," the man said. "Unless you're a fighting man, there ain't no place for you here."

"It sort of sounds that way," McQuaid agreed.

"It's going to be a shooting war any day now," the woman added. "Usta is bragging that he's bringing in a gunman named McQuaid to settle Patzel's hash. Ever hear of McQuaid?"

McQuaid nodded. "Yeah, I've heard of him. But I thought that he had hung up his guns."

"Not according to Cliff Usta," the man said. "I can't

imagine a man like McQuaid taking cards in a little squabble like this."

"Maybe Usta offered him something pretty good," McQuaid said.

"Don't know what it would be unless it would be a piece of the valley, and Usta wants every inch of that himself."

McQuaid had learned more than he had expected to. But what he'd learned had raised as many questions as it had answered. His natural caution warned him not to let these people suspect who he really was.

"I may look elsewhere for work," he said slowly. "My name is Quill, Dan Quill."

The storekeeper stuck out his hand. "Glad to know you, Mr. Quill. My name is George Yount and this is my wife, Polly."

McQuaid acknowledged the introductions. He wasn't so interested in who they were, but he did want them to know who he claimed to be. As free as they were with the information about the Ustas and Patzels, they likely would be equally free in telling everyone who had ridden into the valley.

McQuaid picked up his sack of groceries.

Yount came out from behind the counter to follow him to the door. "Are you going to stick around?"

McQuaid looked thoughtful. "I may ride on up the valley to look around. But this doesn't seem like the kind of setup I want to tie into."

He went out to his horse and took his time about fitting his purchases into the sack of supplies behind his saddle. His bedroll with the necessities of a wanderer's life wrapped inside took up most of the space behind the cantle.

Mounting the horse, he reined away from the hitchrack, aware that both the Younts were at the window, watching every move he made. He wondered if they suspected who he really was. Maybe it didn't make much difference. If he stayed, it wouldn't be long until everyone would know, anyway.

He rode up the street to the north end of town. There the road divided. One fork went straight up the valley, curving slowly to the west to stay on the near side of the creek. The other fork turned across a ford of the creek and went up the far bank. The one that crossed the creek would be the road to Usta's Long Bow Ranch, if he understood things correctly.

Perversely, he held his horse straight up the left-hand road. He wasn't ready yet to talk to Usta. Usta had broken his agreement when he promised McQuaid a deed to land he didn't own. McQuaid wasn't bound now to any promises he had made to Usta.

He had coveted that land up on Hatchet Creek from the day he'd seen it two years ago. He hadn't dreamed then that he'd ever have the chance to own it. Now it was his. It wasn't going to be easy to hold it, but he wasn't going to give it up without a fight.

McQuaid tried to remember exactly what Usta had told him about the situation here. McQuaid had been working in a mine near Central City when Usta had come looking for him.

Usta had tried to hire his gun for the coming fight in Long Bow Valley. But McQuaid had hung up his gun. However, he had learned that he couldn't hang up his reputation. It was that reputation that Usta was trying to hire.

Usta did not discourage easily. He asked what McQuaid wanted for helping in the coming fight. Remembering that pretty little canyon with the waterfall at the upper end, Dan had said he'd take that land never dreaming that Usta would agree. Usta said that he didn't want to part with the land but he'd do it because, if McQuaid didn't help him drive the Patzels from the valley, he might lose everything he owned.

McQuaid had always wanted a place of his own, but he had saved very little money over his wandering years. This looked like his chance to have exactly what he wanted so he jumped at it. Now it looked as if he had jumped at a baited trap. Neither the Patzels nor the Ustas would be obligated to let him live here in peace. They wouldn't do it, either.

McQuaid thought wryly that he probably wouldn't know how to live in peace, anyway. He never had.

The road curved slowly to the northwest, following the bend of the long valley, until it was going almost due west. When he came in sight of the ranches on either side of the creek, he reined up. If he understood it right, that would be Patzel's Hatchet Ranch on the near side of the creek and Usta's Long Bow on the other. They looked as if they were almost across the creek from one another. But he remembered that the Hatchet Ranch had been set up close to the Long Bow because they had been one outfit in the beginning under John Harris. Only after Harris died had the two ranches become enemy camps.

Caution prompted McQuaid to detour around both ranches on his way up the valley to Hatchet Creek. He wanted to look things over before he made any decisions. If they saw him first, those decisions might be taken out of his hands.

Trees marched down the mountains on either side of the valley and crowded out onto the gentle slopes that gave way to the flat grassy bottomland along the creek. McQuaid reined over into those trees and passed quietly beyond the Hatchet ranch house.

He was a quarter of a mile beyond the ranch and was thinking of moving back into the open valley when the small branch of a tree close to his head snapped off.

Even as he ducked, he heard the flat spang of a rifle. Somebody had discovered him. That shot had come within inches of killing him. His hand dropped to his gun.

"Heist 'em!" a shrill voice snapped. "The next one won't miss!"

II

McQuaid hesitated a second, trying to locate the speaker. That hesitation prompted another shot. It missed his head by the width of a whisker, judging from the snap of the bullet.

McQuaid waited no longer. Curiosity wasn't worth it. His hands went up, but his eyes still searched the trees for his assailant. That hadn't sounded like any order he'd ever heard. No one had ever told him to "heist" his hands.

Then he saw why. A slim figure stepped out from behind a tree that he hadn't thought big enough to hide a rifleman. Just a kid, he thought. Over half a foot shorter than he was. Jet black eyes and hair to match. Slim as a willow sprout.

"That rifle's bigger than you are, kid," McQuaid said.

"I'm no kid, mister. Just make a funny move and find out."

It came to him with a jolt and the impression was one he wouldn't forget. This wasn't a kid. This was a grown girl. But that rifle in her hands didn't look any the less formidable because of the discovery.

She was dressed like a boy in a faded shirt and Levi's, worn boots, and a floppy hat that couldn't hide her heavy black hair. Something about the way her sharp chin pointed defiantly warned him not to make an issue of the fact that she was not a boy.

"Do you make a habit of shooting at every man who rides through here?" he asked.

"I do if he tries to sneak around us like you did. Who are you, mister?"

McQuaid thought of the name he'd given the Younts at the general store. "Dan Quill," he said.

The girl looked him over carefully. "You look like you know what a gun is for. Can you handle one?"

McQuaid nodded. "I know which end stings. Do you?"

"Take a look at which end is pointing at you and which one at me."

McQuaid studied the girl. Her sarcasm had a cutting edge. She obviously was as suspicious of him as a mule was of a rattler. But there was no fear in her face. She reminded McQuaid of a gunfighter who had total confidence in his ability to beat anybody who drew on him.

"You must think you're pretty good with that," he said slowly.

She nodded. "Fair. But I'm looking for someone who's better."

He rubbed his chin. "And you think I might be the one?"

"I'm considering the possibility."

"Thinking of drawing on me to find out?" he asked.

"I suppose you wouldn't approve?"

"You're right, I wouldn't. I don't fight women."

Her lip curled. "One of those! Mister, I'm not looking for a knight on a white charger. I'm looking for a gunfighter, one who'll fight no matter who jumps him."

"Reckon anybody would do that," he said.

"Not if he won't fight women. Mr. Quill, what have you done for a living?"

He frowned. "Punched cows, worked in a mine, if it's any of your business."

"It might be. Ever have any gunfights?"

"Plenty," he said. "But not with women."

"I need a fast gun, Mr. Quill. Is yours for hire?"

"No," he said quickly.

Her black eyes bored into him. "You have hired your gun, haven't you?"

"A time or two," he admitted.

She hesitated as if uncertain how to proceed. But McQuaid had no doubt she was going to proceed. He had the feeling he'd have to follow her lead and he didn't like it. He wasn't used to following.

"How long are you planning to be in Long Bow Valley?" she asked next.

"Maybe quite a while," he said.

"You're not passing through, that's sure," the girl said, watching his face closely. "There's no way through Long Bow Valley. It's a dead end. If you have any idea of staying, even for a week, you can work for me."

"I pick who I work for," McQuaid said, anger building at her domineering attitude.

"If you stay, you work for me."

"I'm staying, but I'm working for myself."

"Fair enough," she said surprisingly, "providing you do one job for me."

He shook his head emphatically.

She smiled and he couldn't believe how it changed her looks, even though the smile was a condescending one. She could be downright beautiful. But she could also be downright infuriating as she was right now.

"You're forgetting I've got the rifle in my hand, not you, she said. "I'll give you a choice."

He scowled at her, not even honoring her suggestion with a question. She listened to his silence for only a few seconds.

"You can turn around and ride out of Long Bow Valley, or you can agree to do this one job for me, or you can stay here without a stitch of clothes."

He stared in disbelief. "You're out of your head!"

"Try me and see," she said, keeping the rifle across her arm pointed directly at his middle.

He could see the hammer was back. He didn't doubt that if he balked at her terms, she would either make him strip or she'd shoot him out of the saddle. He hadn't seen anything about her yet to indicate that she would give an inch.

"I'm not leaving," he said slowly. "And I'm not taking off even one boot."

"Good," she said. "That leaves the other choice. You'll do the job for me."

"What job?"

"The Ustas on the other side of the creek have hired a gunman named McQuaid to drive us out of the valley. If you're as good with a gun as you pretend to be, you can handle this McQuaid for us."

"If I hire out to run McQuaid up a tree, what do I get out of it?"

"The right to stay here in Long Bow Valley."

"I was heading for Hatchet Creek," McQuaid said. "I took out papers on some land there."

Her frown deepened, but she didn't back off. "You can stay on Hatchet Creek providing you face down McQuaid."

He wondered if this girl was top boss here. But if she wasn't, he'd like to meet the person who could overrule her.

She motioned with the tip of her rifle barrel. "See that tree over there? Pretend that's McQuaid and see how fast you can center him with your gun."

McQuaid noted that she still kept the rifle on him and she was pointing him the other way. She wasn't giving him any chance to turn his gun on her.

He thought of looking bad with his gun, but if he did, she'd run him out of the valley. While she held that cocked rifle, he had little choice. After all, taking a job to outgun himself should be fairly safe. He could manage somehow to let himself live.

With all the dexterity that he had acquired over the

years, he whipped up his gun and centered it on the tree, but he didn't fire. Glancing around, he saw her smile again. This time it wasn't sarcasm and she was beautiful.

"Not even McQuaid could beat that," she said. "Everybody's heard of McQuaid. He has a great reputation. I never heard of Dan Quill, but I'll take my chances with you."

"Are you ready to take a chance on me without that rifle pointed at my guts?"

She looked sharply at him, then eased the hammer forward and turned the muzzle away from McQuaid. "I thought maybe you knew you weren't good enough to go against McQuaid and would try to get out of it. But you're good enough. I've seen a lot of men handle guns but none like you. How come you don't have a reputation like McQuaid?"

"Maybe I haven't shot the right people."

"You come home with me now. You'll need to know who you'll be fighting with so you won't shoot the wrong person."

"I know McQuaid when I see him. I won't make any mistake. I suppose your family is the Patzels?"

She nodded. "I'm Rocky Patzel. Forgot I hadn't told you. When I first saw you, I didn't figure it was any of your business who I was."

"You seemed to think it was your business who I was," he said.

"You were on our land. That made it my business. Let's go. It's not far to the Hatchet."

McQuaid thought of refusing to go. But he didn't think long about it. That would cause another confrontation. And going along with Rocky Patzel's dream of defending the Patzels from McQuaid might be the easiest way to find out just what he was up against here. Whatever it was, he would have to deal with it sooner or later if he was going to claim the land along Hatchet Creek.

He settled his gun back in its holster, making certain

as he always did that he didn't slam it into the very bottom where it might stick. Then he reined around and followed Rocky.

"How far are we from Hatchet Creek now?" he asked.

"Less than a mile. The mouth of the canyon is only a mile and a half from our ranch." She looked at him. "You'll have plenty of time to look over Hatchet Creek later."

As Rocky led the way into the treeless center of the valley, McQuaid saw that the ranch on the other side of the creek was not directly across from the Patzel buildings. Patzel's Hatchet was farther downstream, but still the two places were less than half a mile apart.

As they rode past the barn, McQuaid saw the small house and the fenced yard. There was no grass in the yard, but there were flower beds. A row of flowers bordered the gravel walk and others snuggled against the side of the house. McQuaid didn't know much about flowers, but he guessed these were petunias.

Rocky and McQuaid got only as far as the yard gate when a man and a woman came out of the house and down the walk. The man was about forty-five, shorter than McQuaid and a little heavier, his brown hair graying at the temples.

The woman was younger with the same black hair that Rocky had. There was no hint of gray in it yet, but lines were beginning to show in her hard face. She was under five and a half feet tall, about the same as Rocky, but she weighed twenty pounds more. Watching her stride down the walk, McQuaid wondered if Mrs. Patzel's sister, over in the Usta household, looked as stubborn.

"This is Pa and Ma," Rocky said. "Meet Dan Quill. A faster gun than McQuaid. I've hired him to face down McQuaid."

Patzel showed surprise, but his wife stared at McQuaid with open suspicion.

"How do you know he's faster than McQuaid?" Patzel asked.

"I saw him draw," Rocky said. "I've never seen anything like it. McQuaid can't be faster."

"It takes more than a fast draw," Mrs. Patzel said. "It takes guts to stand up to a man like McQuaid."

"Ma, he's not afraid of anything. I practically had to shoot him to get him to listen to my offer."

"What kind of wages did you promise him?" Patzel asked.

"No money," Rocky said hastily. McQuaid guessed that money was a touchy subject at the Patzels'. It was probably the only reason they hadn't already hired a man to fight McQuaid.

"What did you offer him?" Mrs. Patzel demanded, suspicion rising in her voice.

"He has papers on that land on Hatchet Creek. I told him we'd let him stay there if he gets rid of McQuaid."

"What?" Patzel roared. "Nobody gets that land but us!"

"It won't do us any good if McQuaid kills us all," Rocky snapped at her father. "I'd rather have Quill for a neighbor than be dead or running for my life somewhere outside Long Bow Valley."

Mrs. Patzel sighed. "She's got a point, Frank. We can't fight McQuaid. Maybe this gunman can."

"But we can't have him on Hatchet Creek, Alice," Patzel said.

The argument between the two died down as three men came from the barn. The Hatchet crew, McQuaid guessed. The shortest man of the three was in the lead. McQuaid tagged him as the foreman, if Patzel had designated a man as foreman for his crew.

The other two were younger. One was taller and heavier than McQuaid with eyes that were muddy brown, almost black, and dark brown hair. Suspicion seemed to be a part of his expression. The other man was just a youngster, not more than twenty, McQuaid guessed. He was slim as a beanpole with soft blue eyes. He looked out of place beside the tall man.

"This is Ollie Heinze, our foreman," Rocky said of the short man. "The tall one is Ed Gideon and the other one is Willy Lintz. Boys, this is our answer to McQuaid, Dan Quill."

Heinze ran a hand through his blond hair and grinned. "We sure need an answer to him, all right. If you can handle McQuaid, you've got my vote."

"Ain't no man can handle McQuaid," Ed Gideon said sourly. "Sure not a soft-looking clown like this."

Rocky's eyes snapped fire. "You'd better shut up, Ed. That kind of talk can get you a pine box and a six-by-three hole. I've seen him throw his gun. You're not in it with him."

McQuaid could see that Rocky's defense of him had made little impression on the tall puncher. He evidently thought himself a fast gun. McQuaid knew that Rocky hadn't spoken out so sharply in defense of him but rather in defense of her own judgment. She had picked him to handle McQuaid and she wasn't going to allow anyone to question her decision.

The youngest of the three Hatchet riders said nothing. There was a look of awe in his blue eyes as he watched McQuaid. McQuaid thought he might like Willy Lintz but he wouldn't trust him. Long ago, he had learned not to trust anyone that he didn't have to. There were fewer disappointments in life that way and far fewer surprises.

Frank Patzel pulled McQuaid's attention away from the crew. "Just how did you happen to decide you wanted that land on Hatchet Creek?"

"I've been looking for some good land to claim for a long time," McQuaid said easily. "I was hunting up in this country a year or so ago. I found out yesterday by accident that this land was open, so I filed on it."

"The land on Hatchet Creek?" Ed Gideon exploded.
"You ain't filing on that, mister."

"I already have," McQuaid said quietly.

"Simmer down, Ed," Alice Patzel said. The tall cowboy snapped his mouth shut as if someone had slapped
him in the jaw. "We've got to have Quill for a while.
Then maybe we'll buy him out."

"I don't plan on selling," McQuaid said.

"You'll sell if we want to buy," she snapped.

McQuaid saw where Rocky got her disposition. But
Rocky was no longer so antagonistic. She was trying to
sell McQuaid to the others so, for the moment, she was
on his side. He liked it that way.

McQuaid was on the point of telling Alice Patzel that
she was a long way from being in a position to tell him
what he was going to do.

But Frank Patzel interrupted. "Almost suppertime.
Better put your gear in the bunkhouse tonight, Quill. You
can headquarter here or up on Hatchet Creek, whichever
you want."

"I'll stay at Hatchet Creek," McQuaid said. He glanced
at the sun and the people around him. "Might bunk here
tonight, though."

Staying at the Hatchet bunkhouse would give him time
to sort out some things. This day had not gone as he had
planned. Heinze motioned McQuaid to follow him toward
the barn and corral. McQuaid fell in step behind him,
leading his horse. He saw Ed Gideon move up to take
Rocky's horse, but Rocky jerked her head angrily and
Gideon backed off. McQuaid read the signs. Gideon had
an eye for Rocky, but she didn't have any for him.
McQuaid had the distinct impression that she had no time
for any man. She was wrapped up in the job she had cut
out for Rocky Patzel and nothing else. He had never seen
a girl quite like her.

Before supper was called, McQuaid lounged on the
empty bunk Heinze had shown him. He watched the other

hands. Lintz sneaked glances at him as he might at a tiger that he was afraid he would arouse. But Ed Gideon was openly hostile. He didn't take off his gun as most cowboys did when they were in the bunkhouse, so McQuaid left his on, too. Something about Gideon warned him of danger. He'd seen the kind before. Sure of themselves and itching to prove their superiority over everyone else.

Gideon toyed with his gun, hefting it as if he were considering buying it in a store. He spun it a couple of times by the trigger guard, always catching it in the palm of his hand, muzzle pointed out threateningly.

"You'd better put that toy away," Heinze said disgustedly. "Willy and me have seen you do that before and I don't figure you're impressing Quill any."

Gideon snorted. "I'll bet he can't even do this." He spun the gun again.

"Can you, Mr. Quill?" Willy Lintz asked softly.

"Never tried," McQuaid said. "You can't kill a man twirling your gun like a button on a string."

"You have to get the feel of a gun if you're going to stake your life on how well you use it," Gideon said condescendingly, looking over at McQuaid.

McQuaid knew that Gideon was not going to stop until he had tested him. He'd seen the kind. Not all of them had been slow with a gun, either. He wondered how fast Ed Gideon really was.

III

McQuaid studied the tall cowboy. Gideon held his gun carelessly in his hand, but the muzzle was almost in line with McQuaid. He couldn't do anything with that gun pointed at him. He wanted Gideon to see his draw. The only hope he had of convincing Gideon not to challenge him in a gun battle was to make him realize he had no chance. And McQuaid wasn't sure he was fast enough to do that.

He got to his feet, walked slowly to the bunkhouse door, and looked out into the yard.

"You ain't got the sense that a gunfighter has to have," Gideon said. "A gunfighter never turns his back on a man with a gun in his hand."

McQuaid turned slowly. "That all depends on who has the gun in his hand. He doesn't turn his back on another gunfighter, that's sure."

Fury rushed up into Gideon's face, tinting it crimson. He held his gun in his hand, but the muzzle was still pointed off toward the bunk where McQuaid had been.

Timing his move precisely, McQuaid whipped up his gun directly in Gideon's face. Gideon jerked when McQuaid moved, but he hadn't done much more than twitch his gun hand when he was staring into the bore of McQuaid's gun.

"A gunfighter never talks a fight," McQuaid said softly. "He just fights."

Gideon simply stared at the gun, saliva dribbling from the corner of his open mouth. His hand pulled away from the gun in his lap.

"Take a good look, Ed," Ollie Heinze said softly. "That's probably the first real fast gun you ever saw. If you keep running off at the mouth, it may be the last one."

Gideon snapped his mouth shut and swallowed hard. He wiped a sleeve across his face, drying off his chin.

"You didn't give me a chance," he said lamely.

"I didn't come here to fight anybody in this crew," McQuaid said. "If I had, they'd be carrying you out now."

Gideon picked up his gun gingerly and dropped it in his holster, then unbuckled the holster and hung it on the nail above his bunk. McQuaid went back to his bunk and hung up his gun belt. Turning, he saw Willy Lintz looking at him, awe and almost hero worship in his eyes. He had made quite an impression on the boy, but he wasn't so sure about Gideon. He'd made Gideon look like a fool and the tall gunman was not one who would accept that role gracefully.

"Quill's on our side, Ed," Heinze said. "Don't forget that." He grinned. "We can find a place for him, even if he ain't a fast gun like you."

"You keep prodding, Ollie, and I'll let you have it," Gideon growled.

"Aw, shut up," Heinze snapped and turned toward the door as the supper call came.

Supper was served in a lean-to at the back of the house. Alice Patzel did the cooking for the crew. She just didn't strike McQuaid as the domestic type, but apparently the Patzels didn't have the kind of money needed to hire a cook for the three-man crew.

Rocky helped carry in the platters of food. She had tied a flour sack over her Levi's and that made her look more like a girl than she had this afternoon.

McQuaid tried to concentrate on his plate and not look at her. But he found his eyes darting up at her as she came through the door between the kitchen and the lean-to. She looked at him only once and he felt like a school-boy caught staring at his teacher.

After supper, he was the first one out of the house. Tomorrow he'd go up to Hatchet Creek and he'd stay there. He'd have to do something about Usta. Usta had brought him here to fight Patzel's outfit. Now that he had seen them, he didn't understand why Usta thought he needed a gunfighter to whip this crew.

Going to his bunk, McQuaid sprawled out to rest until it was time to go to bed properly. He saw Gideon come in, but the tall cowboy ignored him. That was the way he hoped it would stay until he got off the Hatchet Ranch. Ed Gideon was a bitter enemy now, but at least he would be a cautious enemy from here on in. McQuaid knew the tall puncher had intended to work up a fight and kill him just to prove how good he was.

McQuaid had seen such men before. It would take a lot of proving now on Gideon's part to make anyone believe he was a gunfighter. Such a man could be doubly dangerous. A shot in the back wouldn't be beyond him.

Lying there in the growing darkness, McQuaid wondered if he hadn't made a mistake filing on that land. He was going to find it next to impossible just to stay on the place. Between the Patzels and the Ustas, he'd be lucky to last out the week.

On the other hand, this was exactly the piece of land he wanted. Besides, there was Nick Joss's proposition. Joss was a gambler down in Central City, but he had been a prospector before he'd turned to the cards. He still thought like a prospector, always certain he would turn up a bonanza if he just drove a pick into another rock.

He'd heard or seen something about Hatchet Creek that made him certain he'd strike it rich if he could only try his hand in that little canyon. So he'd promised McQuaid forty head of good cattle to stock his place just for the privilege of prospecting in the canyon once McQuaid had settled the war between the Patzels and the Ustas.

Thinking back, McQuaid wondered if he was really cut out to be a rancher. He had never seen his father. He'd been born after his father went off to fight in the War between the States and didn't return. His mother had remarried and his stepfather had dragged the family from town to town all over Kansas. He was a cattle buyer, starting at Abilene, moving on to Ellsworth and Wichita and finally playing out his string in Dodge City. It had been in Dodge City that a man had gunned him down, when his stepson was sixteen.

McQuaid had learned before he was twelve that he had an aptitude for handling a gun. Now, at sixteen, he had gone out to avenge his stepfather's death. He had found the man, challenged him, and beaten him easily. That one incident had stamped him with the brand of a fast gun.

Going south, he hired on to help drive cattle herds north to Dodge City. When Kansas quarantined against the Texas cattle, he helped drive up the trail that followed the Colorado-Kansas line to Nebraska and over to Ogallala. Those were salty crews and McQuaid got into more than one fight that ended with guns. His speed and accuracy with a gun always made him the victor.

When homesteaders fenced off the trails, McQuaid turned to the mountains and the mining towns. Not being much of a gambler, he got a job in the mines. The fights still followed him and he had to prove again that there were few men better with a gun than he was.

His last job at Central City had gone well. He'd put his gun away and had stayed out of trouble. But mining was not for him. He'd seen Hatchet Creek here in Long

Bow Valley and coveted it. And then Cliff Usta had come looking for him. If Usta had had any inducement other than Hatchet Creek, McQuaid could have successfully turned him down. But he'd used the magic words to make Dan take up his gun again.

Now he was here in Long Bow Valley, but the land on Hatchet Creek that was to have been his free and clear for helping Usta drive the Patzels out of the valley was not free and clear at all. He'd had to file on the land and now he'd have to live on it before it could be his. And instead of having Cliff Usta as an ally, he was sure that he'd have both the Ustas and the Patzels as enemies. If McQuaid helped one or the other in the coming fight, he'd still have the winner to whip before he could live on Hatchet Creek in peace.

McQuaid watched Ed Gideon the next morning to see if he had any intention of renewing his attack on him. If he did, they'd have to settle things before he left. But Gideon ignored him as completely as if he didn't exist. McQuaid liked it that way.

Breakfast was in the lean-to again. At least the Hatchet crew ate well, McQuaid thought. As soon as breakfast was over, Rocky jerked off her flour-sack apron. Alice Patzel frowned, but she didn't object.

"I'll ride with you to Hatchet Creek," Rocky announced as McQuaid left the lean-to.

"Going to lollygag after him?" Gideon exploded when they were outside the house.

Rocky turned furiously on him. "I don't lollygag after anybody. You sure ought to know that."

McQuaid grinned. He was already aware of that himself. She had no time for any man unless he could help her in what she wanted to accomplish. She thought McQuaid could help her. She probably had some instructions to give him this morning.

As he saddled his horse, McQuaid thought ahead to

the time when Rocky discovered he was really Dan McQuaid, the man she had hired him to fight. He hoped he wasn't near her when she learned the truth. He had told Rocky yesterday that he had never fought a woman. The time might come when he had no choice in the matter.

"She'll show you what we're up against," Frank Patzel said to McQuaid as he led his horse out of the barn.

McQuaid had planned to saddle Rocky's horse, but he discovered that she already had him saddled. He nodded at Patzel without saying anything. He thought he knew what he was up against. But that certainly wouldn't be the same problem the Patzels were facing.

Ed Gideon watched sourly as McQuaid and Rocky rode out of the yard and up the valley. The Hatchet Ranch buildings were sitting fairly close to the creek, and Rocky angled away from the water as she led the way upstream.

"I want you to understand the situation here," she said in clipped tones like a businesswoman. "The Ustas across the creek are my uncle and aunt. My mother and Aunt Jane are sisters. But Uncle Cliff and Aunt Jane are trying to run us out of the valley so they can have the whole thing."

"Looks to me like the valley is big enough for two ranches," McQuaid said.

"Not when one of them is run by Uncle Cliff," Rocky said. "They hired a gunman named Toby Walsh three months ago. Now they've brought in this McQuaid. You know his reputation."

McQuaid nodded. "I've heard of it."

"One thing you've got to remember. Don't quarrel with Ed Gideon. Other than you, he's the nearest thing we have to a gunfighter. He's not the equal of McQuaid or you, probably not as good as Walsh, but he'll be a help when the fight comes."

"You talk like it's a foregone conclusion that there's going to be a fight."

"What else can you think when they hire gunfighters like Walsh and McQuaid?"

McQuaid nodded. "You've got a point. But with gunmen like that, somebody'll get killed. Is it worth that?"

Her face hardened. "Sure, it's worth it. I'd rather die than let them have this whole valley. With you on our side, we've got a good chance of winning."

"What if I decide to ride out before the shooting starts?"

She shot a sharp look at him. "If you do, you'd better not show your face in this valley again. You won't get that land on Hatchet Creek. We'll see to that if we have to bury you on it."

He didn't doubt that she meant it and, if necessary, she'd try to carry out that threat herself. Both her parents were probably just as determined as she was, too.

"Ever thought of patching up your troubles with the Ustas?"

Rocky snorted. "We were all one outfit while Grandpa was alive. We've been coming apart at the seams ever since. It won't be patched up till one or the other of us is wiped out."

McQuaid had heard the same kind of talk in other range wars where he'd had a part. But he'd never gotten involved in a family fight before.

"That's a no-man's-land," Rocky said, pointing to the creek. "Both our herds water there, but there have been some shots fired across the creek when anyone gets too close. Not much danger of either of us crossing."

"What happens when you meet in town?"

Rocky shrugged. "We don't fight in town. We both have to go there. If we happen to get there at the same time, we ignore each other."

"Better do that all the time," McQuaid said.

"You're getting paid for fighting, not giving advice," Rocky snapped.

"I didn't hear anything about any pay."

Rocky shot a frown at him. "You're being allowed to stay on Hatchet Creek. That's mighty big pay the way we see it."

McQuaid didn't say anything, but it wasn't the way he saw it. Maybe he had joined the right side when he'd first agreed to Usta's terms. The only trouble was, Usta had lied to him and McQuaid had no use for a liar.

As they moved up Long Bow Creek, Rocky pointed out the Long Bow Ranch buildings across the creek. They were no farther back from the creek than the Hatchet Ranch buildings were. A real war could be started by either family while it stayed on its own side of the creek.

Rocky reined up a short distance beyond the spot even with Usta's ranch. Ahead, a stream cut into Long Bow Creek from the left.

"That's Hatchet Creek," she said, nodding at the little stream. "You can pick your own place to camp. Just remember that you're on our side. We'll call you when we need you. And don't forget to stay well back from Long Bow Creek. The Ustas might take a potshot at you any time you get close."

McQuaid nodded. "I'll remember."

Rocky put her horse to an easy lope back toward the Hatchet Ranch and McQuaid turned his attention to the land he had claimed.

At this point, Long Bow Creek ran almost due east between the two ranches, curving to the south farther down until it was flowing almost straight south when it passed the little town of Arrow. Long Bow Valley curved in the shape of a big bow. Hatchet Creek tumbled down the mountains in a long waterfall, then ran through the narrow canyon it had cut over the centuries, finally rippling out into Long Bow Valley to join Long Bow Creek.

McQuaid turned his horse up Hatchet Creek. Trees lined the banks as he approached the mountain that hemmed in Long Bow Valley. The mouth of the canyon where Hatchet Creek ran out into the main valley was narrow, not over fifty yards wide. Just before going into the canyon, McQuaid spotted a high spot on the east side of the creek that was free of trees. That was the spot where he'd build his cabin. It would give him a commanding view of the valley and both the ranches on Long Bow Creek.

Riding through the canyon mouth, he found himself in a wilderness of trees and boulders. The walls of the little canyon were almost perpendicular and up ahead, above the tops of the trees, McQuaid saw the waterfall where Hatchet Creek tumbled down into the canyon. He thought of changing his mind and building his cabin there. It was such a beautiful spot. But he'd feel trapped. He needed open space and freedom.

Suddenly his peaceful mood was shattered by a sharp command only a few feet from him.

"Don't move a muscle, mister. I'd love to have an excuse to kill you."

McQuaid did move a muscle. He turned his head to see who had the drop on him. He had been careless, so carried away by the beauty of the canyon that he had momentarily dropped his guard. A rather squat, heavyset man was standing between two trees, a gun aimed at McQuaid. McQuaid had seen enough gunmen to recognize one on sight. This man was a killer.

IV

The man eased forward, moving quickly, considering his size. "Put your hands on your head," he ordered, "where I can see them."

McQuaid frowned but he obeyed. Men like this one were usually touchy. This entire valley was like a dry powder box. It would take no more than a spark to set it off. It would take a very small spark to touch off this man with the gun.

McQuaid studied him as the man reached up and lifted McQuaid's gun from its holster, keeping his own gun centered on his quarry. His hat tipped, revealing a shiny head as far back as McQuaid could see. His black eyes sparkled with excitement. Guessing the gunfighter was just hoping for an excuse to pull the trigger, McQuaid sat as still as a statue.

After the man had moved around to slide the rifle out of its boot on the saddle, he stepped back, glaring at McQuaid.

"Now that you're dehorned, tell me what you're doing here," he demanded.

"I was just looking over the place," McQuaid said. "Who are you? Do you own this canyon?"

"As much as you do," the man said.

"Since we neither one own it, let's start out by you telling me why you're pointing that gun at me."

McQuaid expected him to balk until he'd revealed who

he was, but the man glared at him a moment, then answered. "I'm Toby Walsh. I work for the Long Bow. I
don't trust any man in this canyon. He might be a Hatchet
man."

McQuaid breathed easier. Rocky had told him about
Walsh, Usta's gunfighter. But the man acted a little un-
sure of himself now.

"I'm Dan McQuaid," McQuaid said.

Instead of relaxing, Walsh seemed to grow more tense.
"So you're the hired gun that Usta brought in. He don't
need another gunhand."

"That could be," McQuaid agreed. "But he hired me.
It might be a good idea to let him know I'm here."

Walsh eyed him for another moment, then nodded.
"I reckon so. But you're not getting your guns back yet.
Not till Usta says you are who you say you are."

McQuaid nodded. He didn't know why Walsh was so
suspicious of him. But he didn't trust him to stand there
holding all the guns while his own most potent weapon
was his imagination. If he could make Walsh take him
to Usta, he'd play it by ear from there.

Walsh backed up to the trees. He reached the reins of
his horse without getting out of sight of McQuaid.
McQuaid didn't even consider trying to make a break.

They rode out of the canyon, McQuaid in the lead.
Following Hatchet Creek to its junction with Long Bow
Creek, they crossed the larger stream and turned down-
stream to the Long Bow Ranch buildings.

Their approach had been seen and it seemed to
McQuaid that the yard was full of people when they rode
in.

"Caught this jasper up in Hatchet Canyon," Walsh
said. "He claims to be McQuaid. I brought him in to find
out."

A tall thin man with graying red hair moved out to the
horses. "That's him, all right," he said.

McQuaid nodded at Cliff Usta. A man back at Central

City had described Usta as a beanpole that had to stand twice to cast one shadow. He was thin, weighing much less than McQuaid although he was two or three inches taller. And McQuaid had always considered himself a trim man.

Walsh dismounted, his squat, heavyset frame a sharp contrast to his boss. "He was snooping around Hatchet Canyon," Walsh said. "Didn't say what for."

"Checking out the land I promised him for helping us wipe out the Patzels," Usta said.

"You ain't really going to let him have that land on Hatchet Creek, are you?" Walsh howled.

"Why not?" Usta snapped. "We need his gun."

"I can outgun any man Patzel has," Walsh said angrily.

"Not saying you can't," Usta said. "But it's better to have two aces when you're playing for big stakes."

"You ain't paying me like that," Walsh grumbled.

"You're getting better paid," McQuaid said. "Usta don't own that land he promised me."

Usta jerked his head around as if McQuaid had hit him with a bullwhip. "Who says I don't?"

"The recorder down at the courthouse at Pinedale," McQuaid said. "Did you think I wouldn't check?"

"If I don't own it, nobody does," Usta said. "It's open for filing."

"I've already filed," McQuaid said. "But that sort of breaks our deal."

Usta held up a hand. "Now hold on. Hatchet Creek was part of Harris's Long Bow Ranch. I never checked to find out if he owned it all legal. We'll protect your right to claim that land. I'll even pay you a wage till this scrap is over."

"Take it easy, Cliff," the older woman in the group said. "I'm not so sure I favor having him there. How are we going to own this whole valley if Hatchet Creek is claimed by a stranger?"

McQuaid looked at the woman. She was almost identical to Alice Patzel. This would have to be her sister, Jane Usta. The same size, black hair, dark eyes, and a stubborn set to her jaw that defied opposition.

"You've got to look at the positive angle," Usta said softly. "Without him, we might not own any part of the valley. Better to have all but Hatchet Creek than not to have any."

"You don't need him," Walsh grumbled.

"I think I do," Usta said.

Usta turned his back on Walsh. "I want you to meet my family, McQuaid. This is my wife, Jane, and my daughter, Bonnie, my sons, Morton and Skip."

McQuaid swung off his horse, thinking he'd rather get his revolver and rifle back from Walsh than meet Usta's family. But that would have to wait. He wasn't in any danger from Walsh while Usta was in charge.

From ground level, his opinion of Jane Usta didn't change. She and her sister were two of the most stubborn-looking women he'd ever seen. But when he switched his gaze to Bonnie Usta, he got a surprise. She was anything but a carbon copy of Rocky Patzel. She was a bit smaller and not so muscular. Instead of having black hair and eyes, she was a blue-eyed redhead. Those eyes were watching his every move now. It disturbed him and he quickly moved his gaze onto the bigger Usta boy, Morton.

McQuaid guessed that Morton Usta was about seventeen years old, a year or so younger than Bonnie. He had some of the height of his father and the dark hair and eyes of his mother. But his eyes were shifty, as if he were constantly afraid someone would see what he was thinking.

The younger boy, Skip, was no more than fifteen. He didn't have the height of Morton but had broad square shoulders. There was a bright defiance in his blue eyes. While Morton was shifty-eyed like his father, Skip was more like his mother, openly defiant. Morton seemed reluctant to approve the hiring of McQuaid but Skip was enthusiastic.

"With Toby and McQuaid, we'll have those Patzels out of this valley in a week," he boasted.

McQuaid realized he was sitting on a keg of dynamite with a lighted fuse. On both sides of the creek, now, they were depending on him to run the other side out. He was thankful that there was no communication between the two camps. But sooner or later, word would filter across the creek that both had hired the same gunman.

A slightly overweight man came shuffling up from the bunkhouse. Usta motioned him over. "This is my foreman, Kenny Coy. Kenny, I want you to meet our new man, McQuaid."

McQuaid met Coy's outstretched hand. Coy struck him as a man with no guile in him. He had a job with which he was satisfied and he'd do nothing to shake the tree.

"I suppose you're happy to have another gunfighter," Walsh said sarcastically.

Coy shrugged, turning to Walsh. "If Cliff says we need another one, that's good enough for me."

"I'm not much of a fighter without guns," McQuaid said. He turned to Walsh. "I'll take back my six-gun and rifle."

Walsh glared at McQuaid, then at Usta. Reluctantly, he handed over the two weapons. McQuaid settled the revolver in his holster, then slipped the rifle back in its boot.

"We're glad to have you with us," Coy said to McQuaid. "I've heard a lot about you."

"We don't need him," Walsh said again to Usta. "I can do the fighting."

"We may not have to do any fighting," Usta said. "Once they know that McQuaid is here, they ain't likely to fight."

"Don't be silly, Cliff," Jane Usta said. "I know Alice and Frank. They'll fight. They'd fight even if you had every gunfighter west of the Missouri on your side."

"Rocky will fight as hard as any of them, too," Bonnie added. "It's too bad she wasn't a boy."

"They've tried to make her one," Jane said. "And you're right. She will fight just like any man."

"I'm not fighting women," McQuaid said.

"You won't have to," Usta said quickly. "If those women over there get into it, I'll take care of them myself."

"Let's see how fast you are with that gun," Skip said excitedly.

"Nothing to be gained by showing off," McQuaid said.

A spark flashed in Walsh's eyes. "Maybe he ain't McQuaid at all. Maybe he's afraid to show how slow he is."

For some reason, Walsh was determined to show up McQuaid. It struck McQuaid that there was a marked similarity between the antagonism of Walsh and Ed Gideon over at Patzel's Hatchet Ranch, but he couldn't see how there could be any connection.

"Don't you think I know who he is?" Usta asked, ruffled at last.

"You know who he said he was," Walsh said. "But did he show you any proof when you hired him that he was really McQuaid?"

Usta frowned. "They told me who he was. No reason for anybody to lie about it."

"He don't look like a fast gunman to me," Walsh challenged. "Make him prove who he is."

"Toby's got a good idea," Skip Usta said, eyes dancing with excitement. "I'll set a couple of bottles up on corral posts. Let's see him draw against Toby. Maybe he ain't who he says he is."

McQuaid was disgusted. He wasn't surprised at Skip. He was just a kid and gunfighters likely were special heroes to him. But Walsh ought to know better. Maybe he just wanted to know if he would have a chance against McQuaid if it came to a fight.

Before Usta could squelch Skip's enthusiasm, Skip had run out behind the bunkhouse, found a couple of bottles in a pile of junk there, and set the bottles on two posts in the corral fence. Running back to the group in the yard, he clapped his hands together.

"Now then at a signal, both draw and see which one breaks his bottle first."

McQuaid didn't like it, but he wasn't going to back down. He could see that Walsh was having second thoughts about it already. But he had gone too far; he couldn't back out. Cliff Usta frowned. He obviously didn't like this competition between his own men, but he, too, saw that it had gone too far to stop.

"I'll count to three," he said. "At three, you both draw and shoot. No cheating. We'll be watching."

McQuaid expected Walsh to use all his speed. McQuaid wouldn't try to be so fast. He knew that too much speed usually resulted in a miss.

So when Usta started counting, he concentrated on that bottle. At three, he drew swiftly but not at his fastest speed. His gun roared almost exactly at the same time that Walsh's did. But Walsh's shot didn't hit anything. Even his second shot didn't hit the bottle. It was his third shot that finally shattered the glass. McQuaid's first shot had splintered the bottle and left the top of the post bare.

Walsh scowled at those around him. "I was just as fast, maybe faster."

"It's not who shoots first that counts," McQuaid said softly. "It's who hits first."

The admiration in Skip's face was proof that McQuaid had made his point. Walsh's face was beet red and his fury almost strangled him. McQuaid didn't doubt that Walsh would have turned his gun on him if he hadn't been convinced by the bottle breaking, too. McQuaid knew he'd have to watch his back from now on. For some reason, Walsh here and Gideon over at the Hatchet wanted to kill him.

"I'll be heading back to Hatchet Creek now," McQuaid announced and swung back into the saddle.

"We'll let you know when we need you," Usta said.

McQuaid rode out, heading for the mouth of Hatchet Creek. He had crossed Long Bow Creek and entered the trees along Hatchet Creek when he heard a horse behind him. Wheeling, he dropped his hand to his gun. But he took it away when he saw Bonnie Usta racing to catch up with him, her red hair flying in the wind. He reined up and waited.

"I haven't been to Hatchet Creek for ages," Bonnie announced exuberantly as she reined up beside him. "Thought this would be a good time to do it and to get acquainted with our new hired man, too."

McQuaid couldn't help comparing Bonnie Usta with her cousin, Rocky Patzel. Rocky was efficient, stubborn, and hard as nails. Bonnie was soft and feminine, giving the impression of helplessness. The one thing they had in common was beauty. McQuaid usually didn't pay much attention to pretty girls. But he had to admit that these were two of the prettiest girls he'd had the fortune or misfortune to run into.

"You've picked the prettiest place in the whole valley," Bonnie said. "I always wanted to build a house over here."

"Maybe you will someday," McQuaid said, not knowing what else to say.

"Show me exactly where you're going to build."

McQuaid welcomed the chance to ride instead of talk. He felt almost tongue-tied around Bonnie. He didn't feel that way around Rocky.

It was the first time McQuaid had actually ridden up on the ridge he had picked out. The view was just as spectacular as he had thought it would be. Bonnie was ecstatic.

"I'm going to come over and see you often just so I can enjoy this view."

"You'll be welcome," McQuaid said, not certain he was telling the truth. He wasn't sure he'd be here long once the Patzels found out who he really was. Hatchet Creek was on the Patzel side of Long Bow Creek. Considering the way the two families felt about each other, he wondered if Bonnie was safe over here now.

"You're quite a ways from home," he reminded the girl.

She nodded. "I know. I'd better get back. I may not see you again for a while unless you go to the dance down at Arrow Saturday night. Morton and Skip and I are going. Are you?"

"I hadn't heard about it before," McQuaid said.

He could see through her scheme. She was hinting for him to ask her to go. But he wouldn't dare risk taking Bonnie Usta to that dance. If Walsh didn't back-shoot him, some of the Patzels would.

"You've heard about it now," Bonnie said. "Don't forget it. I'd better get home."

She turned her horse and headed down Hatchet Creek. He watched her go, thinking that he'd like to take Bonnie to that dance. But he knew such things were not for him now. All he really wanted was a chance to build his cabin and enjoy his land. But he knew there was little chance of that.

While he was still thinking about Bonnie, another rider came up through the trees from the east. His hand rested on his gun until he saw that it was Rocky. He wondered even then if it was wise to relax. Rocky might have seen him with Bonnie.

Rocky reined up ten feet from McQuaid. "I see you didn't take my advice. You're playing with fire."

McQuaid nodded. "You mean Bonnie Usta?"

"That's the most dangerous fire in this valley. What were you doing with her?"

"A man named Walsh got the drop on me here on Hatchet Creek and took me over to the Long Bow," McQuaid said. "Maybe it wasn't such a bad idea to see who the Ustas are."

Rocky, tight-lipped, nodded. "Maybe not. Especially if Walsh had a gun in your ribs. Did you see McQuaid over there?"

He shook his head. "I didn't see him. Walsh and a man named Coy were the only hands I was introduced to."

"Good," Rocky said. "McQuaid isn't there yet. I was afraid he might be." Her eyes turned on him. "You've had your look at them. Now stay away from there. You're fighting for the Patzels. And don't you forget it!"

Rocky turned her horse and headed back down the south side of Long Bow Creek. McQuaid watched her go, knowing he was in a tight spot that was bound to get tighter.

V

Rocky had mixed feelings as she rode back toward the Hatchet Ranch. Dan Quill was a hard man, as bullheaded as she was. They were bound to clash. In fact, they already had. While he hadn't openly defied her, she didn't doubt that he would, especially if she demanded something of him that he didn't want to do. But she really wouldn't want it any other way. A weakling who would bow to every demand made on him would be worthless in a fight like the one coming up.

She glanced back at the knoll she had just left. Likely that was the spot where he intended to build his cabin. That brought up another question. Once this fight with the Ustas was over, if the Patzels won, would Quill stay? Rocky could imagine her mother's reaction if he did. And she was as sure he'd do it as she was that she could read a man like Dan Quill.

Her faith in her ability to handle a man like Quill was not shaken. Somehow she would keep him in line. There was one thing that did worry her, however. Bonnie Usta. She had seen Bonnie leave Quill just before she arrived. What was Bonnie doing over here? This was the Patzel side of the creek.

Rocky did doubt her ability to handle Bonnie. Physically, she could squeeze the life out of her. But Bonnie had a way with men that Rocky had never had. Bonnie could make a man think he was a Greek god even if he was a flunky on a fence-riding crew.

Bonnie called it diplomacy; Rocky called it groveling. She wasn't about to knuckle down and beg for anything. If she couldn't get a man to do something by outright request, she'd either do it herself or let it go undone. She prided herself in thinking there weren't many things a man could do that she couldn't do herself. As she rode out of the trees, she was thinking of the way Bonnie flirted with any man who would look her way.

Ahead she saw Ed Gideon coming toward her. She frowned. Gideon made no bones about his intentions. He was struck with Rocky, but if he had any sense, he'd know he was wasting his time. She certainly hadn't given him or any other man any encouragement. She had a job to do and the only place a man fit into that job was by helping with the fighting to get this valley for the Patzels. Ed Gideon fit into the plan in that respect, but she couldn't get it pounded into his head that his place in this fight was limited to what his gun could do and nothing else.

Gideon reined up and waited for Rocky, then swung his horse around so he could ride beside her.

"What are you doing up here?" he asked.

"Minding my own business," Rocky said shortly. "How about you?"

"I was worried about you getting this far from the ranch," Gideon said. "Nobody from across the creek is to be trusted."

"I know that as well as you do," Rocky said. "But I can take care of myself."

"Just wanted to be sure you were safe," Gideon said.

"Well, you're sure now."

"Are you going to the dance Saturday night at Arrow?" he asked.

"Hadn't thought about it," Rocky said, feeling her anger rise as she guessed what Gideon had in mind.

"We've got more important things to do on the Hatchet than go to shindigs."

"Thought you might like to forget this fighting business for just one night. I'll go along and make sure you're safe."

"I already told you I can take care of myself. If I decide to go, I won't need an escort."

Gideon frowned but still persisted. "Does that mean you won't go with me?"

"That's exactly what it means," Rocky said. "With you or any other man. I haven't got time for that nonsense."

"It ain't nonsense," Gideon exploded. "When I get rich, you'll wish you'd gone along with me!"

Rocky looked at him then. He'd sounded like a little child who'd had his toys taken away from him.

"Just how are you going to get rich?" she taunted.

"I'll do it!" he snapped, his face livid with anger. "Just you wait and see. I know where it is and I'm going to get it."

Her laughter died as she caught something in his voice that chilled her. He glared at her a moment longer, then spurred his horse on toward the ranch.

Rocky kept her eyes on Gideon's back. Just where could he get any money? She was sure that, in his anger, he had let something slip that he hadn't intended to say. But the Patzels didn't have any money so he certainly wasn't planning to rob them.

She rode into the yard thoughtfully. Tying up her horse, she loosened the cinch, then went inside. Her father was in the house, which was unusual for this time of day. Worry over the impending fight seemed to be sapping his enthusiasm for making his ranch prosper.

"Where have you been this time?" Alice Patzel asked from the table where she was kneading some bread dough.

"Up at Hatchet Creek trying to figure out Dan Quill.

I'm sure I saw Bonnie Usta leaving the creek just before I got there."

Alice frowned. "If Bonnie gets her hooks in him, we could lose him."

"I was thinking the same thing," Rocky said.

"Frank, you'd better make Quill stay here on the ranch."

"I don't think anybody is going to make Quill do anything," Frank said, "unless he wants to." He looked at Rocky. "Maybe you could make him want to fight for us, Rocky."

"I'm not going to flirt with him or any other man!" Rocky snapped.

"I didn't say you had to—"

"Let it be, Frank," Alice said. "You're the one who wanted a boy and you've taught Rocky every trick that a boy should know, but you wouldn't let me teach her to be a girl. So don't ask her to be a girl now."

"We need Quill on our side," Frank grumbled. "If Usta gets him, too, we might as well pack up and leave."

"If we had some money to hire him," Alice said, "we'd have a better chance of keeping him. I wish we had some of those nuggets Pa used to bring home now and then."

Frank nodded disgustedly. "If wishes were fishes, all beggars would eat. We can't find where he got those nuggets. I've searched this valley a dozen times."

"Maybe it was somewhere else," Rocky said.

Talk about the gold nuggets her grandfather had found somewhere near here had always fascinated Rocky. If she could just find some of those nuggets, then she could make this ranch into the kind of ranch the Patzels could be proud of.

"He never was gone from home long when he went after those nuggets," Alice said. "So he didn't go far. We always thought he got them in Hatchet Canyon, but we couldn't find the place. Sometimes he'd come in with only one or two tiny nuggets. Other times he came home with several as big as peas. There must not have been many there or he'd have stopped ranching and gone into mining."

"Where there are a few nuggets, there's sure to be a lot of gold," Frank said, his eyes glowing as they did whenever the family talked about John Harris's gold.

"If there had been a lot of gold, Pa would have brought it home," Alice argued. "We weren't rich, you know."

"I know I can find it if we can just get rid of the Ustas," Frank said. "Every time I go up to look in Hatchet Canyon, I run into some of the Ustas."

"They're probably making sure you don't get a chance to do any looking," Alice said.

"I send Gideon or Ollie up there once in a while to make sure they're not looking, either," Frank said. "Now we've got this gunman, Quill, perched right at the mouth of the canyon. They can't even get in to look now."

"Unless they coax Quill over into their camp," Rocky said. "I wouldn't put anything past that flirt, Bonnie."

"I wonder if Jane knows where Pa got his gold," Alice said thoughtfully. "Maybe she got Pa to tell her something he didn't tell me. After all, he did live with her the last two years of his life."

"Do you think your pa made a map of the place?" Frank asked.

Alice shook her head. "I doubt it. But if Jane knows where the gold is, she and Cliff are just waiting till they can get rid of us so they can walk in and get it."

"There wasn't anything in his will about the gold," Frank said.

"There wouldn't be," Alice said. "That would have started a stampede in here and none of us would have got anything. Pa was too smart for that."

"If he hadn't been quite so tight, he would have told somebody where it is."

"If he told anybody, it would have been Jane," Alice said.

"I saw the old man up in Hatchet Canyon several times," Frank said. "I didn't know about the gold nuggets then. He actually ran me out of there once, saying I should be checking the cattle down toward Arrow."

"Maybe you were close to his gold," Rocky suggested.

"I've thought about that since, but I haven't had a chance to really hunt for it. We must get the Ustas out of the valley. Then we'll have time to look for that gold. Now that gunman is keeping us out of Hatchet Canyon, too."

"We'll get rid of him as soon as we win this fight," Alice said.

"He has papers on that land," Rocky said.

"Papers don't mean anything," Frank snorted. "Your grandpa controlled this whole valley, including Hatchet Canyon, and he didn't have papers on anything except the spot where his buildings were."

"Maybe you could get Quill to ride with you into the canyon," Alice suggested. "He could keep all the Ustas away while you looked."

"Don't want him to see me looking for gold," Frank snapped.

"At least, McQuaid isn't here yet," Rocky said. "Quill was taken over to the Long Bow by Walsh. He said McQuaid wasn't there."

"Good," Frank said, his eyes lighting up. "If McQuaid isn't there, this is the time for us to strike. We've got Quill. They haven't got McQuaid."

"Right," Alice agreed enthusiastically. "Hit them before they're ready."

"They've got Walsh," Rocky said.

"We're got Quill and Gideon. Without McQuaid, they can't stand up to us."

"Let's do it," Alice said. "Today. Before dark."

"I'll check things out along the river," Rocky said. "I'll see if they have a guard out. If they have, we'll have to wait till dark."

"Every minute we wait gives McQuaid more time to get to the Long Bow," Alice said impatiently.

"What will we do when we get there?" Rocky asked, wondering just what her parents really had in mind. They'd been talking about this fight for a long time, but this was the first specific aggressive action they had planned.

"We'll burn them out," Alice said without hesitation. "If they'll leave, that's all there will be to it. If they won't leave, then they'll wish they had."

Rocky went outside and tightened the cinch on her saddle. Ollie Heinze came over and asked where she was going. When she told him, he got his horse and rode along. She didn't resent his company like she did that of Gideon. Ollie Heinze treated her like any member of the crew, always had ever since he had come to work here. To Ollie, she was just another boy, not a maverick heifer that needed to be branded.

"Don't like this fighting," Ollie said as they rode toward the creek. "Especially among families."

"They're the ones who want to run us out," Rocky said.

"Seems to me that the wanting is on both sides," Ollie said. "And that Quill must really like a fight to buy into this."

"He was determined to stay. We had to get him before the Ustas did," Rocky said.

"Wonder why he was so set on staying here," Ollie pondered.

Rocky suddenly wondered that, too. Getting a little piece of land hardly seemed that important. But at that instant a rifle shot from across the creek shook her out of her dreaming. Cliff Usta had somebody watching the river to make sure nobody crossed. They'd have to wait till dark and sneak across when they couldn't be seen.

Ollie was already spurring his horse back toward the buildings and Rocky followed him.

"That shot was closer than it needed to be for a warning," Ollie grumbled as he reined up.

Rocky agreed, but she didn't expect anything else from Toby Walsh and she was willing to bet that had been Walsh. But her mind was still on the question Ollie had raised about why Quill wanted to take that land on Hatchet Creek. What did he know that others here didn't? Maybe nothing, and maybe something very important.

She dismounted at the hitchrack. Before she could tie up her horse, Willy Lintz stepped up.

"I'd be proud to tie him and loosen the cinch," he said softly.

She nodded. She tried to ignore it, but she knew Willy had a crush on her, too. She couldn't understand what was the matter with Ed Gideon and Willy Lintz. Maybe it was just that there weren't enough girls to go around, so they concentrated on the ones at hand. And Rocky happened to be unfortunate enough to be handy. At least, she didn't resent Willy like she did Ed Gideon. He didn't look at her as if she were a prize apple ready to be picked off a tree.

Inside the house, she shocked her parents with the question in her mind. "Is it possible that Dan Quill knows about Grandpa's gold deposit?"

Frank's jaw dropped down. "If he does, it would explain why he's so determined to have that land right on Hatchet Creek. He could find that gold and get away before we even guessed what he was up to."

Alice shook her head. "I don't see how he could know. Nobody outside this valley knows about the nuggets Pa brought out."

"Didn't he use those nuggets to buy things?" Rocky asked.

"Just down at the store," Alice said. "Told them he sold some cattle to some miners and they paid him in gold. They believed him."

"We'd better keep an eye on Quill just the same,"

Frank said. "It would be a sad day if we fought a war just to get the right to look for that gold, only to find that somebody else had beaten us to it."

"I'll check on Quill," Rocky said, "and find out if he knows about the gold. I'll make sure he doesn't guess what we suspect."

"Right now, we'd better get Quill down here so we can go after the Ustas," Frank said. "We'll hit them as soon as it's dark since we can't sneak up on them in the daylight. We've got to do it before McQuaid gets to the valley."

Alice agreed. "Send somebody after Quill."

"I'll go," Rocky said. "I know right where he is."

She went back outside, thinking of ways to find out if Quill knew anything about the gold deposits her grandfather had found. Tightening the cinch on her horse, she swung up and headed the horse up the canyon toward Hatchet Creek.

As she rode, she realized that she'd better think about something besides gold. She had to convince Quill to come and fight with them against the Ustas. He hadn't seemed eager to get into this fight, at least not on the Patzel side.

She rode up Long Bow Creek, keeping back far enough to avoid violating the neutral zone. She didn't want to be shot at again. There would be plenty of shooting tonight when the Patzels not only violated the neutral zone on this side of the creek but on the other side, too.

As she rode into the trees that fringed Hatchet Creek, her mind was on the arguments she would use to convince Quill to ride with the Patzels tonight. She didn't see the man at the side of the trail until he leaped out and caught her horse's bridle.

Her hand automatically dropped to the .38 she wore in the holster on her hip just the way her father wore his .45. But the man had a gun in his free hand and he centered it on her. It was then that she recognized Toby

Walsh. He was on the wrong side of the creek, but that didn't decrease the danger to her.

She wondered if he intended to take her over to the Ustas as a prisoner. But he slipped his hand down on the reins and, not letting go of the horse, grabbed her arm and started dragging her out of the saddle.

She prided herself in never showing fear. But this time she gave a short scream before she could check herself. She was afraid of Walsh.

VI

Rocky's scream didn't carry far. But it was far enough to reach McQuaid. He was just leaving the spot where he hoped to build his cabin. He'd been measuring the location and piling rocks at the places where the cabin corners would be.

That short scream stopped him dead in his tracks. He listened and thought he heard a struggle of some kind. Turning away from his horse across the clearing, he ran toward the dim trail that led from the valley to the mouth of Hatchet Canyon.

As he reached the trail, he heard the scuffle again and was surprised to find that he was no more than ten feet from a fight between Toby Walsh and Rocky Patzel. Considering the sizes of the two, it should have been no contest. Walsh outweighed Rocky by at least seventy pounds. But it was a contest and McQuaid wasn't sure that Rocky couldn't win it.

His reaction was violent. Fury washed over him. And with one hand, he grabbed Walsh's arm and tore him away from Rocky, spinning him around like a top. Walsh swore, turned his anger on McQuaid, and charged, swinging a fist wildly.

With Walsh still off balance, McQuaid stepped inside his wide-swinging fist and hammered two blows to the gunman's face. This wasn't McQuaid's style of fighting any more than it was Walsh's. McQuaid wanted to settle this as quickly as possible. If he hurt a hand, he wouldn't be worth much as a gunfighter.

Walsh hadn't recovered from his surprise and McQuaid's fury overpowered him. Those first two blows had taken much of the fight out of Usta's gunman. McQuaid had the advantage and he had no intention of losing it.

Walsh retreated, trying to claw his gun out of his holster. But a sharp order from Rocky stopped him. McQuaid stopped, too, looking around at Rocky, who had her gun centered on Walsh. Walsh eased his hand away from his gun as he faced the girl.

"Get on your horse and get out of here," Rocky snapped, "or you'll be the first one we'll bury in this war."

Walsh obviously believed her for he backed away, glancing around toward his horse. Then his eyes turned on McQuaid, hate brimming over into his face.

"We'll meet on even terms one of these days," he snapped. "When we do, it'll be different."

"We're even right now," McQuaid said. "Rocky'll stay out of it if you want to have a try."

Walsh glared at McQuaid, then flipped his eyes toward Rocky. McQuaid knew then that he was not going to accept his challenge. A gunman never took his eyes off his target if he intended to kill.

"There'll be a better time," he said and spun around, diving through the trees to his horse.

McQuaid turned to Rocky. "Sort of careless letting him get hold of you, wasn't it?"

"I can take care of myself," she flashed back. "No fat pig like Walsh can whip me."

"It's not too smart to give him a chance to try."

Rocky scowled, then pinched back the words she was about to say. When she did speak, her voice was calm again and all business.

"We're going to go after the Ustas tonight. You'll ride with us."

McQuaid frowned. "Hold up a minute. All I agreed to do was to keep McQuaid off your backs. Nothing was said about me riding into this war with you."

"If you want to stay on this land, you'll ride with us tonight," Rocky snapped.

McQuaid's jaw jutted out. "No way!" he shot back. "I agreed to keep McQuaid out of the fight and that's all I'm going to do."

Fury reddened her face. "Aren't you the brave one! You know good and well that McQuaid isn't at the Long Bow yet. So all you have to do is sit up here and laugh while we kill each other. And you expect us to let you stay here on Hatchet Creek for doing nothing?"

"I'm doing what I said I'd do. Nothing more."

Rocky seemed to be struggling with words, fury choking her. Her fists clenched. "We'll have your hide if you don't fight with us," she finally hissed.

McQuaid was as angry now as she was. "You can try," he said. "I'll be right here waiting."

"Are you looking for gold?" she demanded then.

McQuaid stared at her, startled. "I'm no prospector," he said finally. "Even if I was, why would I look for gold here?"

She scowled, confusion showing in her face. "If you won't fight, there just doesn't seem to be any other reason for you being here."

"I took out papers on this land so I could have a place of my own. I intend to stay here and prove up on it, war or no war. Is that reason enough?"

The anger returned to her face. "It seems to be for you. But, mister, you're going to be in this war one way or another. If you don't fight with us, you'll fight against us because we'll run you out. Just bank on that!"

Rocky spun back and swung into the saddle. She

yanked her horse around and presented a stiff back to McQuaid, riding down the trail at a gallop.

He watched her go, wondering why she had asked him if he was looking for gold. Maybe there was something to Nick Joss's conviction that there was gold in Hatchet Canyon.

Watching Rocky disappear down the trail, he thought of Toby Walsh. Would Walsh go back to the Long Bow or would he wait down the trail for Rocky to come along? In spite of Rocky's confidence that she could take care of herself, McQuaid knew that, in an all-out battle, she would be no match for Walsh. He couldn't believe that she didn't know that, too.

Running to his horse, he untied him and mounted, kicking him into a gallop. He slowed down only when he caught sight of Rocky ahead. He stayed far enough behind her so that she wouldn't see him. She was angry enough as it was. If she discovered that he was following her, even to protect her, she'd be mad enough to kill him.

When she broke out of the trees into the open valley, McQuaid reined up. There was no way that Walsh could sneak up on her out there. Evidently he'd had enough for one day after his encounter with Rocky and McQuaid.

Reining around, McQuaid rode slowly back to Hatchet Creek. He couldn't get Rocky's reference to gold out of his mind. The only real hint he'd had that there might be gold in Hatchet Canyon had come from Nick Joss, the gambler back in Central City.

Joss had been in the saloon where McQuaid had met Cliff Usta. He had heard enough of the conversation between Usta and McQuaid to know that some kind of deal had been struck between them and he asked McQuaid about it after Usta was gone.

McQuaid knew Joss fairly well and liked the gambler as well as he liked any man who made his living beating others at cards. He admitted that he might have been a gambler himself if he'd had the knack for it. But he didn't have. Joss did.

McQuaid had told him he had agreed to do some work for Usta in exchange for a piece of land up in Long Bow Valley. Joss showed his knowledge of the country by asking if it happened to be Hatchet Creek.

McQuaid's interest was aroused as well as his suspicions, but he admitted that Joss had guessed right. It was the piece of land he wanted.

Joss had offered to buy McQuaid his supper over at the restaurant so they could talk. Since McQuaid's interest was bubbling now, anyway, he took him up on the proposition.

When Joss found out that McQuaid intended to run cattle on Hatchet Creek, he asked if he could buy into his deal. McQuaid demanded to know why he wanted in.

"That's a fair question," Joss had said, "since I'm not a rancher. But I was a prospector for years. I can find color if there is any to find. Then I discovered that dealing cards was a surer way of raising color. But I still get the urge to try to find the big lode. I was poking around in Long Bow Valley some time ago. Got back into Hatchet Canyon. I found traces of color there. I think there might be something worth digging for."

"Why didn't you go back and look?" McQuaid asked.

"Those two ranchers there wouldn't let me in again. I hear now they are in a war with one another. You hired out to take a hand in that, didn't you?"

McQuaid nodded. "But all I want out of it is that land."

"Exactly," Joss said. "All I want is a chance to poke around in that canyon. I'll make you a proposition: I'll give you forty head of cattle if you'll give me permission to prospect in that canyon."

"Might be a little risky digging around in there while a war is going on."

"Don't plan on digging till after the war is over. This

deal is off unless you're still there on that place when the fighting stops. Then you'll get forty head of breeding stock and I get to poke around at my leisure in that canyon."

"You must be mighty sure of finding something," McQuaid said.

Joss shook his head. "I just want to look. And I figure the only chance I'll have is if you get that land and hang onto it. Forty head of cattle should make it worth your while."

"Don't need any encouragement to make me hang onto that land," McQuaid said. "But if you want to give them away, I'll take them."

"Good enough," Joss said. "I'll be up after the war is over. If you're still there and have a grip on that land, I'll get the cattle for you."

"You can be sure I'll be there unless I'm dead."

Joss grinned. "Don't let that happen. I've got a stake in you now, too."

"Not as much as I have. A piece of land and forty head of cattle sure beats mining."

McQuaid had left Central City with a determination to get that land and hang on. If it had not been for Joss's offer, he might have turned around and gone back when he found that Usta didn't own the land and couldn't give him a clear deed to it. But land and cattle were just what he wanted. He had the chance to get both now and he didn't intend to let it get away from him.

He reined up his horse close to the clearing on the knoll where he intended to build his cabin. He was about to dismount when he saw his horse prick up his ears. Something was near.

Easing his gun into his hand, he stepped out of the saddle and stood by his horse, searching the trees. It might be Walsh coming back to settle the fight that had begun a little earlier.

Then he saw Bonnie Usta riding up the trail. He relaxed. At least Bonnie wouldn't be gunning for him. If that had been Rocky coming, he wouldn't have been so sure.

Bonnie saw him then and reined her horse off the trail into the trees where he waited.

"I was hoping I could find you," she said. "Pa says we're going after the Patzels tonight and he wants you down there by sundown to go with us."

"Why the sudden urge to go after them?"

"We've got you to ride with us," Bonnie said. "Pa thinks maybe we can make them run without a fight."

"You've got Walsh. You don't need me."

"It's because we have both of you that the Patzels should run. Pa says to be there at sundown."

"Tell him not to look for me," McQuaid said.

Bonnie turned a surprised look on him. "Why not?"

"I don't owe your pa anything. We made a deal up in Central City, but that deal fell through because your pa promised to deed me some land he didn't even own. So I'm not bound by any promise I made to him. I reckon he can understand that."

"I don't know," Bonnie said dubiously. "He says he hired you and you promised to fight with us."

"I'll keep my promise when he keeps his promise to give me a deed to this land, clear of all strings."

Bonnie frowned. "He can't if he don't own this land."

"That's why I won't do what I promised."

"But there is more than just Pa involved here. All of us will be run out of the valley if we don't run the Patzels out first."

"What else can he offer me to fight for him?" McQuaid asked.

"I don't know," Bonnie said.

"Why didn't he come himself to try to get me to ride with him tonight?"

"I wanted to come," Bonnie said, smiling shyly. "I told you I liked it up here and I'd come every chance I got."

McQuaid wasn't so sure that Cliff Usta hadn't sent Bonnie because he knew he couldn't persuade McQuaid to fight after tricking him like he had. Maybe Usta thought Bonnie had other means of persuading him to come. McQuaid had to agree that Bonnie herself was a mighty strong argument. He'd consider it a privilege to do a lot of things for a pretty girl like Bonnie. But not this. He wasn't going to get involved in a war just to please a pretty girl. He'd turned down one, Rocky. And she was just as pretty as Bonnie, but maybe not as sweet-tempered and enticing.

Bonnie sighed. "I'll just tell Pa you won't come. Are you going to be at the dance in Arrow tomorrow night?"

"Hadn't figured on it," McQuaid said. "I don't know anyone around here."

"A dance is a quick way to get acquainted," she said. "I'd sure be proud to introduce you around."

"Will the Patzels be there?"

"Not likely. Uncle Frank and Aunt Alice are too old to go, I guess. And Rocky just don't go any place where the boys can get their hands on her."

"And you don't mind if they get their hands on you?"

She shrugged. "Not if it's the right boys. Better think about it. We'd have fun there."

"I've got a cabin to build," McQuaid said.

"You can't build a cabin in the dark. The dance is at night. So is the raid tonight." Her face lost its smile. "You can't just sit up here and not take sides. This fight takes in everybody in the valley."

McQuaid didn't doubt the accuracy of that. But he was going to stay out if he could. He watched silently as she reined her horse around and rode back to the trail leading down to Long Bow Creek.

VII

Bonnie turned once to look back but the trees were thick and McQuaid was not out on the trail so she couldn't see him. She had told the truth when she'd said she loved this location. She didn't know why her grandfather had picked that spot down on Long Bow Creek to build when he could have built up here where he'd have had a commanding view of the entire valley.

She thought back over what she had said to McQuaid when she had been up there. She hoped she hadn't said too much. It was easy to get carried away sometimes and say something that would backfire later.

She couldn't think of anything she had said today, however, that would cause her trouble. She had been very careful not to let anything slip that McQuaid could interpret as meaning the Ustas had no intention of letting him stay on that piece of land once the fighting with the Patzels was over.

She knew it had never entered her father's mind that the Patzels might win this fight. Cliff Usta just didn't lose. He had hired Toby Walsh to assure the Ustas of victory. Then some time after Frank Patzel had hired Ed Gideon, he had gone out and found Dan McQuaid. Cliff Usta always made sure he had one more ace in his hand than his opponent before he laid any money on the table.

He had made a bad mistake with McQuaid, though.

When he had found out that McQuaid wanted this piece of land, he had promised it to him. Of course, he had no intention of letting him have it. That wasn't his mistake. His mistake had come from not anticipating that McQuaid might check at the courthouse to see if the land really belonged to Cliff Usta. The odds had been long that he wouldn't. But Dan McQuaid was a careful man. That was why he was still alive and the men he had fought were not.

Bonnie was disappointed that McQuaid had refused to ride with the Ustas tonight, but she wasn't surprised. If McQuaid had gone with them tonight, they could have driven the entire Patzel family and crew out of the valley, either from fear or by force. Either way, by tomorrow morning, the Ustas would have had complete control of the valley and been free to explore Hatchet Canyon at will.

She thought of McQuaid as she did every new man who showed up. There weren't too many, just those that her father or Frank Patzel hired to take part in the coming fight. She was more interested in the men as men, not as warriors. And Dan McQuaid rated high in her estimation. Tall, slim, with gray eyes and sandy hair, he was as handsome as a Greek god in her opinion. She wanted to think of him as a friend, not an enemy. As a friend of the Ustas, he would be around where she could talk to him and try to attract him as she had others. Somehow she felt he would be more of a challenge.

Coming out of the trees, Bonnie saw that Toby Walsh was at the creek near the spot where she would have to cross. Toby was on the Usta side, but she had no desire to try her wiles on him. The same was true of Ed Gideon over on the Patzel side of the creek. He frightened her. But not Willy Lintz. She would like to know him better. Maybe she would see him at the dance tomorrow night. The Hatchet crew was usually there. At least Gideon and Willy were.

Arrow was the only place where Bonnie got to see the men from the ranch across the creek. Out of necessity, the two families had an undeclared truce in Arrow. Both had to buy things at the store so they couldn't fight there. At least not until one had the definite advantage.

Walsh waited at the creek until she had crossed. She saw the anger in his face even before she reached him.

"Have you seen McQuaid?" he demanded.

Bonnie shrugged. "That's what I went over there for."

"If you had a chance to kill him and didn't, you ought to be horsewhipped."

"Why?" Bonnie demanded angrily. "He's on our side."

She watched the emotions work in his face. He hated McQuaid with a passion and she didn't know why. If McQuaid was fighting for the Patzels, she could have understood it. Maybe he was jealous. Walsh considered himself a fast gun. But there was no doubt that McQuaid was better. He had proved that.

There was something else. Walsh had never confided in her or any other member of the Usta family. But Bonnie was sure that Walsh had something on his mind besides fighting the Patzels.

"McQuaid has to go," Walsh growled. "He's just as liable to kill us as them."

"I don't think he's going to fight on either side," Bonnie said.

"Cliff says he's being paid to fight for us," Walsh said. "What kind of a double-crosser is he? We'd better kill him now before we're all sorry we let him live."

"After we get rid of the Patzels, we'll see about McQuaid," Bonnie said.

"We'd better take care of him first."

"No," Bonnie said sharply. She didn't usually clash with the hired help like this, but Walsh, for some reason, was determined to go gunning for McQuaid right now. The plans were to go after the Patzels tonight. If McQuaid wouldn't come to help, they'd certainly need Walsh.

"We wouldn't have to watch our backs if he was dead," Walsh growled.

"He won't shoot you in the back. He wouldn't have to. And don't you get any ideas about bushwhacking him. Pa says he gives us a definite edge over the Hatchet crew."

Walsh nodded grudgingly. "All right. We'll take care of him later."

"Only when Pa says so," Bonnie reminded him.

She doubted if he heard her. If he did, he gave no heed. She didn't know what Walsh had in mind but it meant trouble for McQuaid. She had watched men close enough in her few years to be able to predict some of their moves. She'd warn McQuaid the next time she saw him, although she doubted if he needed any warning.

Walsh headed for the barn and corrals while Bonnie rode on to the house. She didn't unsaddle her horse. She might need him in a hurry. There was no way of knowing what might happen after the first gun was fired tonight.

Cliff Usta met her as she came in the door. "What did he say?" he demanded.

"He balked on helping us," Bonnie said.

"Balked?" He followed her into the big living room, which was the coolest room in the house. "You should have told him we'd roast him alive if he didn't help us."

"He knows that," Bonnie said. "He claims you lied to him about the land. Says he doesn't owe you anything he promised you."

Cliff frowned. "I never expected him to check on those records," he grumbled. "He's too snoopy for his own good."

"You just got caught in one of your tricks," Jane Usta said. "He strikes me as a pretty sharp hombre."

"He'll fight!" Cliff growled. "We'll find a way to make him fight."

"He may fight for the Patzels if we push him too hard," Jane suggested.

"He won't fight for Frank!" Cliff roared. "He'll fight for us."

"You'd better ride up there and tell him that," Jane said.

"Nobody tells a man like that anything," Cliff said, calmer now.

Bonnie read the signs. Her father was thinking now. His initial burst of rage was gone. He wasn't like her mother. Jane Usta would have barged up there and told McQuaid exactly what was what and demanded that he fall in line. Cliff Usta never met any problem head-on if there was a way to sneak up on its blind side. He was looking for a blind side to McQuaid now. Bonnie doubted if McQuaid had one.

"We'll do something to McQuaid and make it look like the Patzels did it," Cliff said finally, his forehead furrowed in thought. "If he's sure that one of the Patzels tried to do him in, he'll come running to our side."

"That might work," Jane admitted grudgingly. "But I think he'd understand it better if you told him plain out where he stood."

"He'd understand that we need him worse than he thinks we do," Cliff said. "That sure wouldn't convince him to join us."

"Better let Toby do whatever you're planning," Jane suggested. "If McQuaid is half as good a fighter as I think he is, you might wind up with a broken head."

Cliff shook his head. "Not Toby. He'd either get killed or kill McQuaid himself. He wants him dead for some reason. We need both Toby and McQuaid."

"If he killed McQuaid, we wouldn't be any worse off than we are now since he won't help us," Jane said.

"If we have both Toby and McQuaid on our side, even Frank might think twice before he opens up a war with us."

"Frank ain't opening up the war," Jane reminded him. "We're doing it. Tonight."

"Don't blow your hat off," Cliff warned calmly. "If McQuaid don't ride with us tonight, we may wait another day or two. Frank ain't going to get any more gunmen. We can strike anytime as long as we've got McQuaid."

"What are you going to do, Pa?" Bonnie asked. She understood her father much better than she did her mother. Trickery was always better and safer if a person could make it work.

"Call Morton in here. He's the one to help figure out what to do."

Jane yelled and both Morton and Skip came in from the other part of the house. Morton had the sly ways of his father. Bonnie also preferred the clever schemes of her father to the forcefulness of her mother. And she had her father's red hair and blue eyes. Jane often said she was her father's girl.

"Mort, I want you and Bonnie to do some thinking on a scheme to bring McQuaid around to seeing things our way. He's balking on helping us tonight."

Morton nodded. "We'd better not hit them without McQuaid."

"Already decided that myself," Cliff said. "But if something happened to McQuaid and he thought it was the Patzels who did it, he might see the light."

"I reckon," Morton said, grinning.

"Why not just tell him what to do and make sure he does it?" Skip said.

"Shut up, Skip," Cliff said. "You'll get yourself killed before you're dry behind the ears." He turned to Bonnie and his older son. "Now I'm banking on you two to figure something out."

"We'll do it," Bonnie promised.

"Is it possible that McQuaid knows something about that gold in Hatchet Canyon?" Jane asked. "He seems determined to squat right there at the canyon mouth."

"There's no way that he could know about that," Cliff said.

"He sure wants that land on Hatchet Creek awful bad," Skip said.

"He does, all right," Cliff admitted. "But there's no proof that the gold your grandfather found was in that canyon."

"We always thought it was there," Jane said. "But he wouldn't tell a single one of us where he got those nuggets."

"We're sure not going to waste any time looking for that gold till we get Frank and his outfit out of the valley," Cliff said. "Hatchet Creek is on their side of Long Bow Creek. They would claim it if we found anything."

"They'll be gone in a few days," Jane said. "Then we'll get that gold."

"Could any of the hired hands on either ranch know about it?" Bonnie asked, thinking about Toby Walsh and her conclusion that he was after something more than just a chance to fight the Patzels.

"Never thought of that," Cliff said, obviously surprised by the notion.

"Pa never let it leak out about his gold," Jane said emphatically. "Not even Ma or us girls ever found out where he got those nuggets. We just knew that he was finding them somewhere in the valley."

"That's enough to open up a gold rush," Cliff said. "And it sure has opened up a war between us and Frank's outfit."

"You want that gold more than I do," Jane snapped.

Cliff nodded. "Maybe so. And we'll get it in the end, too." He looked at Bonnie and Morton. "Maybe you could cause something to happen at the dance tomorrow night that would convince McQuaid that the Patzels are out to get him and he'll have to join us to save his own skin."

"Only trouble with that idea is that he isn't going to the dance," Bonnie said.

Cliff shrugged. "There's more than one way of getting

somebody to go someplace he hadn't planned to go. Use your brains, girl."

"There is a limit," Jane said sharply.

"Don't worry about me, Ma," Bonnie said. "Mort will be with me. We'll figure something out. In fact, I don't think we'll even go to see Mr. McQuaid. But we'll get him to that dance."

Jane shook her head, but Cliff only grinned. Bonnie nodded at Morton and they went outside to their horses. Bonnie was glad she hadn't unsaddled her horse. She had use for him now. Morton followed without a word. He'd do what had to be done, but he'd depend on her to do the thinking.

VIII

As evening approached, McQuaid's alertness increased. He wasn't sure what to expect from either the Ustas or the Patzels. Both had demanded that he help them tonight and he had refused. They were not accustomed to being turned down. Their reaction might be sudden and violent.

He knew there were two men down there, at least, who would rather kill him than enjoy a good meal. Neither Walsh nor Gideon would hesitate at shooting from ambush, he was sure. He wondered if he could survive here while those two were unshackled.

Nor did those two gunmen tell the entire story. Rocky Patzel and both her parents would not hesitate to come after him if they got angry enough. Over on the Usta side, it was Cliff Usta that McQuaid was most wary of. Usta wouldn't face McQuaid in an open fight, but he was tricky. He'd proved that when he'd hired McQuaid with a promise of some land he didn't own. He might resort to worse trickery than that to get his way. And there was no doubt that both Usta and Patzel were depending on McQuaid's help in this fight.

He found a small clearing in the trees below the knoll. Here he could keep out of sight of anyone in the valley and yet be able to see both ranches. If there was a battle down there tonight, he wanted to see it. He wondered

on which side of the river it would be fought. Each side
had said it was going to raid the other.

Although he waited until nearly midnight, watching
till dark, listening afterward, he saw and heard nothing
out in the valley. Apparently the battle hadn't materialized. Wondering if the entire war between the Ustas and
the Patzels was just a lot of words, he went back to his
camp at the edge of the clearing. He staked out his horse
in the best grass on the knoll and went to sleep.

He was a light sleeper and thought once he heard a
sound. Moving himself up on an elbow, he tried to see
across the clearing, but there was a cloud over the moon
and he couldn't see anything. He laid awake for half an
hour listening but heard nothing more and decided it was
nerves that was giving him false warnings.

Sunrise found McQuaid getting his breakfast. The light
of day gave the clearing a beautiful peaceful look that
belied his imagination of the night before. But when he
finished his breakfast and started across the clearing to the
spot where he had staked out his horse, he discovered
that the horse was gone. He hadn't been able to see that
from the place where he'd cooked his meal.

Hurrying forward, he looked into the trees, hoping
that the horse had simply pulled his picket pin and wan-
dered off. But the horse was nowhere in sight. Examining
the spot where the pin had been driven into the ground,
he could see that it had been pulled straight out. The
horse could not have done that. Someone had stolen the
horse.

Anger washed over him. This must have been in retaliation for his refusal to go on that raid last night. But
which outfit had done it? He had refused both of them.
His first thought was Rocky. She was not one to take a
slap in the face without striking back. But would she
steal his horse in retaliation?

In long strides, he headed for the Hatchet Ranch, a
mile and a half away. If his horse was at Patzel's, he'd

have to determine whether it had been stolen by someone from the Hatchet or left there by someone who wanted him to think they had stolen it.

He wasn't sure what kind of greeting he would receive at the Patzels' but, in the mood that engulfed him now, he didn't care much. The entire family and crew seemed to be waiting for him as he approached. He looked around for his horse but didn't see him.

Ollie Heinze, at the corral, was first to meet McQuaid. Ollie stared at him a minute.

"You look half naked without your horse," he said. "How come you're walking?"

"I was thinking I might find out here," McQuaid said. "Somebody stole my horse last night."

Heinze frowned. "We ain't horse thieves."

"Somebody is," McQuaid said. "I thought the thief might have come from here."

Heinze turned and matched McQuaid's stride up to the yard gate where Frank and Alice Patzel had joined Rocky, who had been talking to Willy Lintz. Ed Gideon came from the bunkhouse.

"Anybody here steal a horse last night?" Heinze asked, his voice suggesting how ridiculous he thought the idea.

"We've got all the horses we need," Frank Patzel said. His eyes flipped to Rocky. "You didn't move his horse just for spite, did you?"

"If I was going to spite him, I wouldn't take it out on his horse," Rocky snapped.

McQuaid saw the anger in her face but not guilt. She hadn't taken the horse. If she was going to do anything to give him trouble, it would probably be right before his eyes. Stealing was not her way.

Heinze turned to Gideon. "How about you, Ed? You didn't git sticky-fingered last night, did you?"

"I never left the bunkhouse and you know it," Gideon said.

"That's right," Heinze said. "Same for Willy." He

turned to McQuaid. "I reckon that clears the Hatchet."

"Maybe," McQuaid admitted. "But my horse didn't wander off by himself."

"I don't take kindly to being accused of stealing a horse," Gideon said angrily, glaring at McQuaid. "You'd better produce facts before you start pushing, mister."

McQuaid eyed him steadily. "I'm looking for facts. Somebody stole my horse and I intend to find him if I can. Don't you start pawing the ground unless you've got a reason."

Gideon glared at McQuaid but said no more. Rocky moved up to face McQuaid then.

"I don't appreciate being accused of horse stealing, either."

"Do you think I appreciate walking?" he demanded. "What happened to that raid you were going to make on the Long Bow?"

"You ought to know," Rocky snapped. "You were to ride with us. We'll go when you go with us."

"That may be a long time," McQuaid said. "I'm going to look for my horse."

He turned and strode out of the yard. He hadn't seen any guilt in anyone there. Heinze vouched for Gideon. McQuaid trusted Ollie Heinze. And the same went for Kenny Coy over on the Long Bow. Those two foremen had obviously been hired when the ranch owners were not thinking of fighting. Neither foreman was a gunfighter.

Once out of sight of Patzel's Hatchet Ranch, McQuaid moved into the trees, then down Hatchet Creek and across Long Bow Creek. From there, he made his way to Usta's Long Bow.

There was a reception committee here, too, but it didn't include everyone on the ranch. Cliff Usta was in the yard, along with Bonnie and Toby Walsh.

McQuaid watched Walsh closely as he approached. The man was dangerous if given an advantage. McQuaid didn't intend to give him that. He announced his reason for being there and watched faces. Walsh showed some satisfaction and amusement, but there was no trace of either guilt or pride. He probably hadn't taken the horse.

Neither Cliff Usta nor Bonnie were as easy to read as Walsh. There was no obvious guilt in their faces, but seldom did a gambler let his face reflect the kind of hand he held. Both Cliff and Bonnie could put on what McQuaid called poker faces.

"I'll help you look for him," Bonnie said, concern in her voice. "You're not going to be able to do much till you get your horse back."

"That's right," McQuaid agreed. "I thought maybe someone here was mad enough to steal my horse because I wouldn't go on the raid last night."

"Hardly," Cliff said easily. "There are better ways of showing our anger."

"Why didn't you go on that raid?" McQuaid asked.

"I hired you to help us drive the Patzels out," Cliff said. "I figure I ought to use you now that you're here. As soon as you see the light and side with us, we'll push them out. Then you can live in peace up there on Hatchet Creek."

Cliff Usta hadn't said it in so many words, but it was clear that McQuaid wouldn't be left in peace until he did join Usta in his effort to move the Patzels out. It was what he had expected.

"He ain't got any right to live anywhere in this valley in peace," Walsh growled.

"Any time you figure on doing something about that, you let me know," McQuaid said.

"No fighting," Bonnie said quickly. "Toby just doesn't like the hint that he might have stolen a horse."

"I'm not accusing anyone," McQuaid said. "Just looking for my horse."

"If I find any trace of him, I'll let you know," Bonnie promised.

McQuaid turned back toward Hatchet Creek. He'd see if he could find a trail from the clearing. He should have looked this morning, but he'd been sure that someone on one of the ranches had stolen the animal. He wasn't entirely convinced yet that they hadn't.

It was almost noon by the time he got back to the knoll near Hatchet Creek. He made two complete circles around the clearing. The only tracks he found were in the pine needles and could have been made by his horse any time when leaving this clearing. Whoever had taken the horse had led him away right over the trail McQuaid had used. They knew the country or else they were very clever horse thieves.

He came back to his supplies and got out his grub. He cooked his dinner and was just cleaning up his place when he heard a horse coming. His hand was on his gun as he waited. For an instant, he thought it might be his own horse coming back. But it wasn't.

Bonnie rode into the clearing and directly across to McQuaid. She reined up.

"I've got good news for you, Dan," she said. "Morton rode into Arrow this morning and he saw your horse there."

"Who's got it?"

"I don't know," Bonnie said. "The horse was tied to the corral fence behind the pool hall."

McQuaid frowned. "Why would anybody steal a horse, then tie him to a fence right in town?"

Bonnie shrugged. "I can't see any reason why anyone would steal your horse at all. Tying him up in town isn't any crazier than stealing him."

McQuaid smelled an ambush. When he went after that horse, someone would be waiting for him. It was too obvious. Everyone knew a man without a horse was the same as a cripple. He'd go after his horse because he had to have him. But who would be waiting for him?

"Could be a trap," Bonnie suggested. "Tell you what.

I'll get an extra horse and ride into town with you. If somebody has any idea of bushwhacking you, he'll think twice if I'm along."

"If it happened to be one of the Patzel crew, say Ed Gideon, he might shoot you, too."

She looked startled. "Maybe. But I'll take the chance. I'm going into town, anyway. Tonight is the dance in Arrow."

McQuaid frowned. "You don't expect me to go to that, do you?"

"Why not? You'll be in town, anyway. That is, if we can dodge an ambush."

McQuaid felt suspicions washing over him. But he had to have that horse. And Bonnie was offering him a Long Bow horse to ride into town. He didn't like the prospect of walking the five and a half or six miles into Arrow.

"It's a deal," he said finally. "But I don't want you riding close enough to me to get shot if someone is laying for me."

"I don't figure on letting you get shot now," Bonnie said and reined around. "I'll be back pretty soon with a horse."

It was an hour before sundown when Bonnie brought McQuaid a horse. They rode back past the Long Bow Ranch and stayed on that side of the creek on their way to town. He kept alert as they rode but saw no sign of trouble.

They found McQuaid's horse tied to the corral fence behind the pool hall. McQuaid was very cautious about approaching the horse. He checked every doorway and building corner nearby. There was no sign of an ambush. That only increased his vigilance.

He watered the horse, for he had no idea how long he had been standing there with nothing to eat or drink. After feeding him at the livery barn, he led him up to the dance hall and tied him in front. A crowd was gathering. It was obvious that these Saturday night dances were a big thing in Arrow.

Bonnie was waiting for him so they could go in together. This seemed to be a personal triumph for her. Inside the door, McQuaid halted to look over the crowd. Since the ambush hadn't materialized yet, maybe it was waiting for him here.

He saw Morton and Skip Usta along one wall. The music hadn't started yet and it was a time for visiting. But he saw one group visiting that shocked him. Toby Walsh was in the far corner and with him were Ed Gideon and Willy Lintz of the Hatchet. McQuaid jerked his head at them.

"What do you make of that?" he asked.

Bonnie's brow pulled into a frown. "I don't know. Of course, we do have a truce here in Arrow. No fighting between anybody from the ranches. But we sure don't visit like old friends."

"Looks like they are," McQuaid said.

The music started and reluctantly, McQuaid went out on the floor with Bonnie. He looked over the crowd for the Patzels. But he didn't see any of them. Only the Hatchet hired hands were here.

McQuaid and Bonnie got into a square with Walsh and some girl McQuaid had never seen.

"Did the cry-baby get his horse back?" Walsh said softly as he joined hands with McQuaid in accordance with directions from the caller.

"The next time that horse is stolen, the thief won't walk away," McQuaid replied.

McQuaid felt the animosity in both Walsh and Gideon. There was a truce here in Arrow, but it was between the Long Bow and the Hatchet. McQuaid wasn't included.

More people arrived and the floor became crowded. Plenty of people from beyond Long Bow Valley came to these dances, McQuaid saw. It soon got hot and stuffy inside.

"Maybe we'd better get some fresh air," he suggested to Bonnie and she agreed.

Outside, Bonnie led the way to one corner of the building where the night breeze stirred the air. Just as McQuaid stepped up to the corner, a heavy blow hit him on the side of the head. Even as he reeled backward, the thought flashed through his mind that this was the trap he had been expecting.

IX

McQuaid caught himself against the side of the building. Fist fighting wasn't his strong point. He dropped his hand to his gun. But two more men charged around the corner of the meeting hall and engulfed him.

His right arm was pinned back against the building while quick fingers pulled the gun out of his holster and tossed it against the wall several feet away.

It was dark and the fists pounding at him gave him no chance to identify his assailants.

It ran through his mind that this beating might be the real reason for getting him to Arrow. Fury surged up in him. He swung a fist as hard as he could and got some satisfaction out of the solid jolt when he connected with someone's ribs. It brought a grunt and the man retreated. But he came back after catching one breath.

McQuaid knew he was going to lose this fight. There were too many against him—three, if he was counting right.

He took one sledgehammer blow on the side of the head that made things whirl. He kicked at the man and hit him on the shin, bringing a howl of pain. McQuaid gritted his teeth against the pain of the beating he was taking. His real regret was that he couldn't dish out as much punishment as he was getting. He knew he was going to go down soon.

Two more heavy blows smashed into his face, one

from either side. His head felt as if it had been caught in a slamming door. Lights flashed before his eyes. Then things went dark. He felt himself sliding to the ground.

He fought to retain consciousness. Dimly he was aware of Bonnie's voice, almost a scream. He clung to the edge of consciousness and hunched back against the wall. They weren't beating him anymore and his vision had cleared enough so that he could see Bonnie holding a gun and forcing the men back around the corner.

When they were gone, she dropped on her knees beside him. "Are you all right, Dan?"

"Never felt better," he mumbled through bruised lips.

"No bones broken, are there?"

"I hope not," McQuaid said, pulling himself painfully to his feet. "Who was that?"

"Ed Gideon and Willy Lintz," Bonnie said.

"I counted three," McQuaid said, wiping a sleeve across his face, sure that it was covered with blood.

"They probably hired someone to help them. Cowards usually do that. They can hire a man at one of these dances for the price of a drink."

"Where did you get that gun?" he asked, pointing to the revolver she was still holding.

"It's yours. I saw where they tossed it when they took it away from you. I got it as soon as I could work around to it. I don't know what they might have done if I hadn't got this gun."

She handed the gun to him and he dropped it back into his holster. He was feeling better now, but it would be quite a while before he felt good again.

"You'd better get back to your dance," he said.

"I'm not going back in there," Bonnie said. "I'm going to help you get home."

"I'm just as well off here," McQuaid said. "The best I can do at my camp is wash myself off in the creek. There's a creek here."

"I can do better than that," Bonnie said. "I'll get some medicine from home as we go by and fix you up."

"Guess I could use some fixing up, all right," McQuaid agreed.

"The Patzels must have stolen your horse and brought him to town just to get you here where they could beat you up," Bonnie said.

"Logical," McQuaid agreed. "But which one would plan that?"

"Gideon," Bonnie said quickly. "Or maybe Uncle Frank. Even Rocky might have done it if you crossed her."

"I crossed her, all right," McQuaid said. "But I don't think she'd set up a trap like this. If she got mad enough, she'd come gunning for me herself."

"That's probably right," Bonnie agreed. "But one of them did. We ought to go after the Patzels right now."

"Not with me in the crowd," McQuaid said. "I couldn't lick a banty rooster now."

Bonnie sighed. "I guess that's right. You'll need some rest now. But it makes me so mad when I think what they did to you."

"If they wanted to keep me out of a fight for a while, they did a good job."

McQuaid walked unsteadily toward his horse. His head was clearing rapidly and he was sure that he'd recover quicker than he had let Bonnie think. As he reached his horse, Morton and Skip Usta came from the door of the hall.

"What happened?" they demanded of Bonnie.

Bonnie explained quickly. "I'm going to take him home now."

"Is he still balking at fighting with us?" Skip demanded.

"He's too banged up right now to think what he wants to do," Bonnie said. "But he knows it was Ed Gideon

and Willy Lintz who beat him up. They hired someone
to help them."

"Maybe we'd better plan on taking the Patzels apart
about tomorrow night," Morton suggested. "By then,
McQuaid ought to feel up to going with us. He's got a
mighty good reason now to get into this fight."

"Reckon I have," McQuaid said. "But I'm not about
to get into any fight till I feel different than this."

McQuaid got back on the horse he had ridden down
to town. Bonnie mounted, too. Then she took the picket
rope of McQuaid's horse and led him. McQuaid thought
it was odd that neither Skip nor Morton offered to come
along with their sister and lead the horse. But they returned to the dance. He wondered if there was any real
affection among the Usta children.

It was a slow trip up the east bank of Long Bow Creek.
McQuaid felt better with each mile, but he didn't let
Bonnie know. He had a lot of puzzles to figure out. At
the Long Bow, Bonnie stopped and got some medicine
and bandages. Then they rode on to the clearing next to
Hatchet Creek. McQuaid helped get a fire started.

By the light of the fire, Bonnie said they'd be going
on a raid tomorrow, and they'd need him. She dabbed
on some medicine that stung, then wrapped one cut on
his neck with a bandage.

"The rest will just have to heal in the fresh air," she
said. "You'd look like a mummy if I wrapped all those
cuts and bruises."

Bonnie took the Long Bow horse back and McQuaid
staked out his horse close to the saddle and bridle beside
his own blankets. They wouldn't steal him again without
his knowing it.

After Bonnie was gone, he thought about Walsh and
Gideon talking together at the dance. Maybe this whole
war was just a sham. But if it was, why had Cliff tried
to hire him to help the Ustas? It had to be a real war, but
Walsh and Gideon apparently didn't take it too seriously.

It was more than just a truce in town that had allowed them to talk together so amiably.

Sunday morning found McQuaid as stiff as a spavined horse. He was still puzzled over last night. Why had Gideon and Lintz jumped on him at the dance? He had decided yesterday morning that Gideon had been surprised when he'd said his horse had been stolen. Had he been mistaken about Gideon? Maybe it had just been an act on his part. Or maybe it hadn't been Gideon and Lintz who had jumped him last night. If he could be sure who had beaten him up last night, he'd likely know who stole his horse the night before. It had all been part of a trap.

Moving around his breakfast fire, McQuaid tried to loosen up stiff muscles. By the time the sun was up an hour, he felt much better. He'd have a sore face for a few days and exercise wasn't going to help that. But the muscles in his arms and shoulders that had taken such a pounding in the fight were becoming less painful as he moved around.

He was considering saddling his horse and riding around, more to ease the remaining stiffness in his joints and muscles than to go anywhere, when he heard a horse coming through the trees along the south side of Long Bow Creek. He stopped, his hand close to his gun. At least this wasn't a surprise attack. The rider was making no effort to keep quiet.

Then he saw Rocky riding toward him into the edge of the clearing. And when she got close enough so that he could see her face, he realized that stealth was the last thing on her mind.

She reined up and stared down at him. "You're a sight!" she said angrily. "I hope you learned to keep your hands off things that can burn you."

"Was that the reason why you had them jump me?"

"Me?" she exploded. "I wasn't at that shindig."

"I didn't say you were," McQuaid said. "But those jaspers who jumped me had orders from somebody."

"And you think I sent somebody down to Arrow just to rough you up?" She laughed shortly. "If I had wanted you roughed up, I'd have come down and seen to it myself. And you wouldn't be walking around this morning, either."

"How come you know so much about it if you weren't there?" McQuaid demanded.

"Willy told me."

"You didn't send him down?"

"Willy and Ed and Ollie work for us. Saturday night is their own time."

"Didn't recognize any of them," McQuaid said. "But there were three."

Fury built up in Rocky's face. "Are you trying to say that the Hatchet men beat you up?"

McQuaid squinted at her. "Didn't they?"

"No!" she snapped. "Willy said you got beaten up, but he didn't say who did it. He did say who you took to the dance, though."

He nodded slowly. "So that's why you're on the warpath."

"If you're going to help the Ustas, say so and we'll come gunning for you. We like to know who our enemies are."

"It looks like I'm everybody's enemy," McQuaid said. "But I'm not fighting for Usta."

"Bet you didn't tell Bonnie that."

"I didn't tell her anything."

"I suppose you took her to the dance out of the kindness of your heart," Rocky said sarcastically.

"I didn't take her to the dance at all. I went to Arrow because she told me my horse was down there and I went after him. She went along."

"And I suppose you found your horse on the dance floor?"

"No," McQuaid said disgustedly, ''he was playing the fiddle! Look, I don't care whether you believe me or not.

My horse was in Arrow, but I don't know yet who stole him."

"How do you suppose Bonnie knew he was in Arrow?"

"She said Morton saw him there."

"I'll bet he did!" Rocky said sharply. "It's hard to put something somewhere without seeing it."

McQuaid studied Rocky's face. She could be right. It could have been an Usta trap. It had been Bonnie who had said that it was Gideon and Lintz who had beaten him up. They had been at the dance, he knew. But Walsh and Morton and Skip Usta had been there, too.

"I saw Walsh and Gideon talking together last night like buddies," he said, sidestepping the doubt she had raised. "Any idea what they'd have to discuss?"

Rocky's face suddenly took on a puzzled frown. "They should have been shooting at each other," she said. "Of course, there is a truce in Arrow between the Hatchet and Long Bow. But there's no buddying. I'll talk to Ed about that."

"You won't learn much," McQuaid said. "If he was up to some mischief, you'd be the last one he'd tell."

"You don't like Ed, do you?"

"Any reason why I should?" McQuaid asked. "He's a puffed-up smart aleck. You'd be wise to watch him."

Rocky straightened, as if dismissing the subject. "We're going after the Ustas tonight, with or without you. If you value your hide, you'll be with us."

"I do value my hide," McQuaid said. "That's why I'm not mixing into this scrap on either side."

"Hatchet Canyon is on our side of Long Bow Creek. We control things over here. You'd better take a good look at which side of your bread has the jelly on it."

Rocky wheeled her horse and kicked him into a lope across the clearing and into the trees. McQuaid watched her go, then turned back toward Hatchet Canyon. He needed to think if he were going to avoid being dragged into this fight. He wanted to look over Hatchet Canyon on foot, anyway. Maybe there was gold here. Nick Joss seemed to think so.

He had other things to think about, too. Rocky had implied that the Ustas had stolen his horse to draw him into town where they could beat him up. Of course, that would be Rocky's defense when he accused the Hatchet crew of doing it. On the other hand, maybe the Ustas thought he would fight on their side if he believed it had been the Hatchet men who had beaten him up. That scheme fit his opinion of the way Cliff Usta would fight.

Tonight he'd stay away from both ranches and find out whether this was just a word war or whether they meant business.

He moved up the creek slowly, looking for any signs of color in the sand or water. Just a few yards short of the pool at the foot of the falls where the creek tumbled down into Hatchet Canyon from the plateau above, he saw what he thought might be a speck of gold.

Stooping down, he touched the sand with his finger. The color disappeared. He didn't know much about gold, but he'd guess there was a little here. Nick Joss had probably seen something like this that made him think he could get rich quick if he were just allowed to prospect for a while in this canyon.

McQuaid moved up closer to the falls. He didn't see any more color until he reached the pool. Seeing a tiny speck of yellow, he dropped to his knees.

It was then that a rifle spanged and the bullet slapped into the water in front of him. McQuaid threw himself backward, jerking up his gun as he did. He saw the rifleman almost instantly and recognized Toby Walsh. Walsh had no business over on this side of Long Bow Creek. McQuaid knew he was at a distinct disadvantage—his revolver against Walsh's rifle. He was in a tight spot.

X

Toby Walsh was angry. It must have been buck fever that had made him miss that first shot. But he still had Dan McQuaid at a real disadvantage. He fired the rifle again but knew he'd missed the second he squeezed the trigger. McQuaid had dodged over behind a rock at that very instant.

McQuaid's revolver was barking and Walsh was within its range. Walsh had a healthy respect for McQuaid's marksmanship. He didn't want to get into an even duel with him. He couldn't forget how McQuaid had shattered that bottle on the corral fence on the Long Bow with one shot that afternoon while it had taken him three shots to do the same thing.

A twig snapped off just above Walsh's head as he started to peek around the tree trunk to see where McQuaid was. He had to get back out of range of that revolver. If he didn't, he might never get out of this canyon alive.

There was a side gully leading down to the creek just behind Walsh. He threw himself backward into that gully, then turned up, away from the creek. Keeping low, he put distance between himself and McQuaid. But there wasn't much room in this narrow canyon to maneuver. When he reached the canyon wall, he was still within long range of McQuaid's gun.

Dodging behind the thick trees along the wall, he worked his way down to the mouth of the canyon where he had left his horse. He'd seen McQuaid come in here on foot and he had been sure this was the day he'd get him. But he'd missed his chance.

At a break in the trees, Walsh looked back. He couldn't see McQuaid. He considered trying to finish the job now. But he knew the risk. There'd be a better time. He wouldn't miss next time.

Reaching his horse, he mounted and put him through the mouth of the canyon and down Hatchet Creek. McQuaid was a hard man to kill. Walsh had faced several men over smoking guns and he was still alive to tell about it. But McQuaid was something else. Maybe it was his reputation. Walsh had drawn his gun as fast as McQuaid that day at the Long Bow. The difference had been that McQuaid had hit his target on the first shot. Walsh hadn't.

Walsh wouldn't admit that he was buffaloed by McQuaid. But when he reached the showdown with him, he was going to make sure he had the advantage. None of this fair-play business. That was for dead heroes.

But somehow he had to get rid of McQuaid. It really didn't matter how. He thought that he had his chance last night when Bonnie had asked him to help Morton and Skip beat up McQuaid. They were to keep their identities hidden so she could blame the Patzels for the attack. That was a ridiculous way to get a man to fight for you, he thought. But he hadn't cared whether McQuaid was fooled or not. He had hoped to kill McQuaid before the fight was over. He hadn't planned on Bonnie getting McQuaid's gun after he'd thrown it aside and using it to stop the fight. Of course, that made her look good in McQuaid's eyes and Walsh had an idea that was important to Bonnie.

If she had just given him another minute, he'd have broken McQuaid's neck. This morning he had thought he would catch him so stiff and sore that he couldn't handle himself well. He'd had every intention of finishing him off. He didn't care who they blamed for it.

Then, after trailing McQuaid into the canyon, he'd missed that first shot! Walsh had never missed such an easy shot before. Missing his first two shots at that bottle the first day McQuaid had showed up still preyed on his mind and it might have given him the shakes just as he squeezed off that shot this morning.

There had been something else in the back of Walsh's mind, too. McQuaid was poking along the creek. Was he looking for the gold? There really was no other good reason why he had filed on that particular piece of land. He must know about it. It was a matter of the success of Walsh's scheme to get rid of McQuaid before he did find that gold.

Walsh rode on to the Long Bow. After dinner, he'd go to his secret meeting and they'd work out something.

All the Ustas, including Bonnie, were loafing around. Cliff Usta never asked his crew to work on Sunday. But today they were planning for their raid tonight across the creek.

Skip Usta looked up as Walsh rode in. "Where have you been?" he demanded.

Walsh scowled. He didn't like any of the Ustas except Bonnie. And he wouldn't like her if she wasn't a girl. But Skip in particular got under his hide. He was as bossy as his mother.

"Been up to see how McQuaid survived his little scrap last night."

"What did you find out?" Bonnie asked quickly.

Walsh frowned at her. "You doctored him up real well. He's ready for anything again."

"Good," Bonnie said. "I told him we'd need him tonight."

"Did he promise to come?" Cliff asked.

"He didn't say he wouldn't," Bonnie hedged. "He believes it was Gideon and Lintz who beat him up. So he won't help them."

"I figure McQuaid is in this just for himself," Walsh said. "If he fights for anybody, it'll be because he sees a big profit in it for himself."

"Everybody does that," Cliff said. "Even you."

Walsh shot a sharp look at Cliff. But Cliff wasn't even looking at him. Walsh let his breath out slowly. He didn't dare show his alarm. Nobody knew what he was working for and he didn't dare let them suspect.

"Dan wants that land, nothing more," Bonnie said.

Walsh turned his attention to Cliff Usta. "We've got to get rid of that gunfighter right away. From the tracks in the wet grass up at his camp, I'd say he had company this morning from the other side of the creek. I'll bet he'll ride with them."

"I'll bet he won't," Bonnie said quickly.

"I'll string along with Bonnie," Cliff said. "She knows men better than either one of us. We need him tonight. After that, we'll talk about getting rid of him. I agree that we can't leave him sitting up there on Hatchet Creek after we get the Hatchet outfit out of the valley."

"I thought Toby was going to kill him last night the way he was pounding him," Morton said. "We were just to beat him up and lay it on the Hatchet."

"That's all we did," Walsh growled. "But I ain't sure he took the bait."

"Bonnie says he did," Skip said belligerently.

Walsh didn't say anything. He would argue with Cliff or Morton or Bonnie. But he knew better than to argue with Skip. Skip would argue for a while. Then he was ready to fight. Walsh didn't doubt that he could kill Skip in a gunfight. But he wasn't ready yet to break with the Ustas.

Jane called Bonnie into the house and the men got

ready for dinner. Walsh ate hurriedly. He didn't want to be late for his appointment. There would be no work around the ranch this afternoon except getting ready to ride against the Patzels after dark. Walsh was ready for that right now.

Announcing that he was riding down to Arrow, Walsh got his horse as soon as he was through eating. Cliff warned him to be back before sundown and he promised he would be.

Walsh rode down the valley until the creek curved to the south out of sight of the ranches. Here he crossed the creek and rode up the slope into the trees to the southwest. In the trees next to a jumble of rocks that had tumbled down from the cliffs long ago, Walsh dismounted. He had gotten here first.

He waited only a few minutes, however, before Ed Gideon rode through the trees to the rocks.

"Where's Willy?" Walsh demanded.

"Wouldn't come," Gideon said. "Claims he doesn't feel good. If you ask me, I think he's showing a yellow streak."

"We shouldn't have asked him in," Walsh said thoughtfully. "But we need every man we can get."

"He knows too much now," Gideon said. "We've got to keep him."

"You're right. But we'll watch him. If he shows the white feather when we get to the showdown, we'll put him out of his misery fast. I reckon he'll stick, though. He likes gold as well as any of us."

"Are you sure there is gold in Hatchet Canyon? We're doing a lot of work for nothing if there ain't."

"Of course, I'm sure," Walsh said. "Sutter told me about it. He worked in the store in Arrow when Old Man Harris brought in gold nuggets to trade for supplies. Harris said he got the gold as payment for cattle sold to miners. But Sutter said Harris hadn't taken any cows out of the valley, so he knew he hadn't got the gold from any miners."

"Maybe he found it somewhere outside the valley," Gideon suggested.

"He found it in Hatchet Canyon," Walsh said positively. "The old man ran Sutter out of that canyon one day with a gun. He never bothered him anywhere else on the ranch. I've found color in that canyon myself. Once we have time to look, we'll find the lode."

"Will we have to change our plans any?"

Walsh nodded. "Enough to get rid of McQuaid immediately. He's in our way. Not only that, but I think he's onto the gold up in that canyon, too. He was poking around the creek this morning. I tried to get him, but I couldn't get a good shot and I missed."

"You mean you had a chance to kill him and missed?" Gideon exploded.

"Don't get edgy about it!" Walsh snapped. "You've had as many chances to kill him as I have. And I don't see you wearing his scalp."

"We can't wait any longer to kill McQuaid if he has his eye on that gold."

Walsh nodded. "You're on target now. The thing is, Cliff is planning a raid on the Hatchet tonight. I think he's going through with it this time."

Gideon nodded. "Frank's planning a raid on the Long Bow tonight, too. That's going to be some show with each outfit starting out to raid the other one."

"It gives us the chance we've been waiting for," Walsh said. "It might work out fine for us if McQuaid will just join in the fun." '

"I ain't sure he'll join us. Rocky looked plenty mad when she got back from talking to him this morning."

"Bonnie says he'll ride with us," Walsh said. "But I ain't half as sure of that as she and Cliff are. I hope he does. He'll be my first target when the shooting starts."

"If he's on our side, I'll get him. What about the rest of our plan?"

"Same as it was. We've got to get rid of both families. Then if we can get the valley for ourselves, fine. But whether we do or not, we'll have the chance we need to search Hatchet Canyon for that gold."

"We ought to be looking now," Gideon complained.

Walsh shook his head. "Don't be a fool, Ed. If we located the gold now, somebody would find out. And you know whose gold it would be. Either Patzel's or Usta's, not ours. Once they're out of the valley, though, nothing can stop us from getting the gold for ourselves."

Gideon sighed. "I hope so. What about Willy after we find the gold?"

"We won't need him once we get rid of the Patzels and Ustas. We can eliminate him then easy enough. But right now, we've got to keep him on our side. If we don't, he'll fight for Patzel and that will mean one more man we'll have to whip."

"We're still outnumbered even with Willy on our side," Gideon said.

"We won't be much longer," Walsh said confidently. "Vinny Niccum will be showing up one of these days. Now there is a real gunman. Not even McQuaid can lick him. Besides, if we have any luck tonight, the odds will be in our favor even before Niccum gets here."

"Then we won't need him."

"Maybe not," Walsh said slowly. "But we'll wait and see how we make out tonight. Wiping out two families ain't going to be easy."

"Just how are we going to go about it?"

"Our targets tonight are McQuaid first, then Frank Patzel and Cliff Usta. You knock off the head of a snake and there isn't much bite left."

"There are the two old ladies," Gideon said. "They're both scrappers."

Walsh nodded. "I know. But we can lick a couple of women."

"Make that three," Gideon said. "Rocky is a worse fighter than either one of the others. Morton won't be any trouble. But Skip might be."

"I'll handle Skip," Walsh said. "In fact, I'll enjoy that. He's a bossy kid and I've just been waiting to put him in his place. Six feet down."

A rattle in the jumble of rocks jerked Walsh's head around. He saw nothing, but something had dislodged a rock in that pile at the foot of the cliff. He drew his gun. What if somebody had heard them talking? He had chosen this place to meet because it was far from either ranch and also a long way from Arrow. There shouldn't be anyone here.

"What is it?" Gideon whispered. "A badger or a squirrel?"

"Maybe," Walsh said. "But we sure have to find out." He motioned Gideon to the right, while he turned around the left side of the jumble of rocks.

Moving silently, Walsh began circling the rocks. He heard more rocks rattling again ahead of him, but he continued his slow progress. If it was an animal, there was no danger. But if somebody had heard what he and Gideon had said, he'd have to be shut up.

Keeping his eyes on the rocks, Walsh moved around to the point where he thought the rocks had fallen. There was nothing there. Then out of the corner of his eye, he caught a movement and whirled. A man was just disappearing into the trees near the bluff twenty yards from the rocks. If Walsh hadn't been concentrating so hard on the rocks where he'd heard the noise, he surely would have seen him sooner.

Whipping up his revolver, he fired once. But he knew he had missed even as he squeezed the trigger. Gideon came dashing around the rocks, climbing over the last few that were jammed against the cliff.

"Who was it?"

"Not sure," Walsh said. "I think it was that kid who freights stuff from Pinedale to Yount's store."

Gideon took a deep breath. "I'm glad it wasn't somebody from one of the ranches."

"Doesn't make any difference who he is," Walsh snapped. "We've got to get him. He'll tell somebody what he heard if we don't. Get your horse."

Walsh turned and dashed toward his horse with Gideon at his heels. Swinging into the saddle, Walsh reined downstream. The kid must have a horse back in those trees somewhere. They had to cut him off from the horse and corner him against that cliff.

He heard Gideon behind him as he guided his horse between the trees. Then he saw the kid running hard toward a horse another fifty yards ahead. The kid apparently had just come up for a ride and had decided to hike a little. Walsh realized he hadn't meant to eavesdrop. He'd just happened to be sitting in those rocks when Walsh and Gideon came.

But that didn't change anything. He'd heard too much. The success of Walsh's scheme depended on nobody knowing. It was the kid's tough luck that he had overheard what he had.

Walsh cut the distance between him and the kid to a few yards. Finally the kid turned a terrified face toward Walsh and stopped running, his hands in the air. Walsh and Gideon reined up.

"Now what?" Gideon asked.

"This," Walsh said. Quickly he fired two shots. The kid crumpled in his tracks. Walsh glanced at Gideon and saw the disbelief in Gideon's face.

"There wasn't any choice," Walsh growled. "If he'd got to anybody, he'd have told what he heard. Our plans would have been mud." He reined around. "Now that the ball is started, let's go get McQuaid. He's the one we have to kill if we're going to get what we want."

Gideon reined around, but his head swiveled to stare at the boy's body. Walsh wondered how tough a hand Gideon really was. He'd known that Willy Lintz wasn't much of a fighter. Now he had doubts about Gideon.

They reached Hatchet Creek by staying in the trees along the mountain slope. Walsh motioned for silence as they approached the clearing where McQuaid had his camp.

Reining up within sight of the clearing, he searched the area. Little prickles ran up his spine. McQuaid wasn't in sight. But he was like an Indian. It was when you didn't see an Indian that you needed to be afraid.

"I don't see him," Gideon said softly beside Walsh.

"I don't either. He may be back in the canyon again."

"Or he may have us in his sights right now," Gideon said nervously.

Walsh nodded. "He's tricky. We'll do better to figure out where he's going to be and lay an ambush for him."

"You're right. We sure ain't going to gain nothing if he beefs us."

Without another word, Walsh reined around and headed back through the trees. He didn't like the feeling about this place. McQuaid gave him the creeps, anyway. So far, he hadn't been able to touch him. Walsh had the feeling that it would always be that way and he didn't like it. He'd lay a trap and kill McQuaid. But this wasn't the moment for it.

XI

McQuaid was watching every move that the two men made. He recognized Ed Gideon, but a tree blocked his view of the other rider. Since they were on the south side of the creek, he had to assume that it was Willy Lintz.

One thing didn't seem right. Lintz didn't strike McQuaid as the kind who would sneak in with the deliberate intention of killing him. These two had. The cautious way they had approached and their halting just within sight of the clearing were as easy to read for McQuaid as if they had shouted their intentions from the top of the mountain behind him.

He had heard them coming because he had every nerve tuned for danger. If they had ridden into the clearing, he'd have had them in his sights. But they reined around and went back, their enthusiasm apparently fading.

He shifted around as the riders left, trying to get a better view of the man with Gideon. From the back, it looked more like Toby Walsh than Lintz. But Walsh had had his try at McQuaid this morning. If that was Walsh with Gideon, it suggested a much closer tie between the two than he had guessed from seeing them talking at the dance last night.

One thing was certain. Neither ranch was friendly to McQuaid. They would feign friendship as long as they thought they had a chance of getting his help in the coming fight. But once that was over, no matter which way it went, that friendship would be gone.

After tonight, whether or not the planned raids came off, McQuaid would be a marked man on both ranches because he wasn't going to help either side.

As the sun dropped behind the far peaks, McQuaid moved down to the fringe of the trees overlooking Long Bow Creek. This was as close to the fighting as he intended to get. Coming down here would also give him first look at anyone from either ranch coming to make a last effort to get him to join them tonight.

Somehow he wouldn't be surprised if nothing happened out there. It hadn't the other night when they'd planned their raids but aborted them when he refused to join either side. The situation was identical tonight.

As darkness deepened, McQuaid moved out of the trees and down to a clump of water willows he had seen along the south bank of Long Bow Creek not far from Usta's Long Bow buildings across the creek. If anything happened, he should be able to see it from here.

The moon, three quarters full, was well up in the eastern sky. It would be a fairly bright night. McQuaid watched the Long Bow for activity. Usta had the most men, counting his own sons. But there were more fire-eaters on the Patzel side of the creek. Frank Patzel, his wife, Alice, and Rocky were all determined to win this battle. Cliff Usta was not so belligerent even though his wife, Jane, was.

McQuaid wasn't surprised when he saw riders leaving the Hatchet Ranch. They were so far away from his hiding place that he could barely make them out. But their movement rippled across his vision as they headed for the creek. They apparently intended to cross near their own buildings, then move up the north bank of the creek to the Long Bow.

There was activity on the Long Bow, too. This was

close to McQuaid. He couldn't make out the individuals, but he saw them mount up out by the corral. They started for the creek, then suddenly turned around to the east to face the riders coming at them.

This was the battle they both had anticipated, although McQuaid was willing to bet this wasn't the way either had expected it to be fought. Each had planned to surprise the other and lay a siege.

Rifles started barking long before the two groups came together, and the advance of both outfits halted. Men dismounted and continued firing, using their horses for protection.

It became obvious within a minute that this was not to the liking of either side. There would be several killed if this kept up. While both sides had declared their eagerness for the battle, neither wanted to risk any losses in the process.

The actual battle lasted no more than five minutes. The Patzels were the first to begin a slow retreat. McQuaid couldn't be sure, but it looked from this distance as if one man was being held on his horse while the others backed off on foot, leading their horses. It appeared that the time was ripe for the Ustas to charge forward and put the Patzel outfit to flight. Instead, the Ustas began a retreat of their own.

McQuaid watched them, looking for any sign of wounded among them. Every man seemed to be walking all right and leading his horse. The Patzels, when the engagement had been completely broken off, mounted and rode across the creek to the Hatchet buildings.

McQuaid slipped out of his hiding place and back into the trees along Hatchet Creek. If ever there had been an inconclusive battle, that had been it. He wondered if it would have been different if he had been with one of the outfits.

Tempers on both ranches were bound to be hot now.

McQuaid went to the clearing and moved his supplies
back into a cove in the bluff where he didn't think they
could be found in the night. Then, leading his horse, he
went into Hatchet Canyon. He had spotted some fine
glades of grass earlier and he staked his horse out in one
of them. Then he lay down in the trees, well protected
from any prying eyes but still where he could see his
horse. Satisfied he had done all he could to protect himself and his things, he dropped off to sleep.

He awoke at dawn. The peacefulness of the canyon
almost lulled him back to sleep. In the morning light, he
saw that he had picked a very secure spot. He wanted
to keep it that way so he could use it again, so he took
his horse back to the clearing outside Hatchet Canyon
and got breakfast there. He kept a sharp eye on the
ranches. He expected trouble from them now since he
hadn't fought for either side last night. Probably neither
the Ustas nor the Patzels knew that he hadn't been with
the other side.

The first stir came from the Patzel ranch just as he was
finishing his breakfast. A rider left the corrals and came
straight up the valley. McQuaid moved across the clearing so he'd be close to the rider when he came in sight
through the trees.

He wasn't surprised when he saw Rocky. She jerked
back on the reins when she spotted him. Her face was
flushed with anger.

"So!" she snapped. "You decided to fight with your
beloved Bonnie!"

McQuaid held up a hand. "Hold on. I told you I wasn't
going to fight with either side. I didn't. They're probably
just as mad over at the Long Bow as you are."

"I doubt it," she said, the fury not abating in her face.
"They didn't lose anybody on their side."

McQuaid remembered the man who was being held
in the saddle last night. "Who did you lose?"

"Pa was shot. He ain't hurt too bad, but he won't be fighting for a while. So we're shorthanded. That's why we backed off."

"And you thought I was with Usta?"

Her head came up. "Yes, we did. If it'll make your head swell any bigger, we thought your gun gave them too much power for us. If we'd known you weren't there, we might have stayed with it."

"And somebody else would have been shot," McQuaid said.

"If you'd been with us, Pa wouldn't have got shot. We'd have run them out before they had time to do any damage."

"Just having me along wouldn't have made that much difference," McQuaid said. "Might have not made any difference at all."

McQuaid had been so intent on watching Rocky that he hadn't noticed the approach of another rider. He heard the other horse at about the same time Rocky did. She backed her horse off into the edge of the trees. McQuaid would see the visitor before she did.

The visitor's coming up through the trees along Hatchet Creek meant that it was almost sure to be somebody from the Long Bow. McQuaid thought of Walsh but discarded that instantly. Walsh wouldn't be making that much noise. It had to be Bonnie. She wouldn't be afraid of McQuaid. Walsh was.

Bonnie rode into the clearing, her eyes sweeping around the area. When she saw McQuaid, she headed toward him.

"Dan McQuaid!" she called. "Where were you last night?"

McQuaid whipped his eyes to Rocky still on her horse but only five feet away. At the sound of his name, her eyes widened in astonishment. That gave way instantly to an even greater rage.

"So you're McQuaid, not Dan Quill!" she hissed.

Her hand slapped the gun at her hip, but McQuaid was on that side of the horse and, in one giant step, he was close enough to grab her hand before the gun was out of its holster.

"Put it back," he snapped.

She ignored him and struggled to get the gun out where she could use it. McQuaid abandoned words and wrenched the gun from her hand and stuffed it under his belt. She tried for her rifle next. He grabbed the butt of the rifle at the same time she did. Again his superior strength wrested the weapon from her hand.

"Now then, you listen for a minute," he said angrily.

"You traitor!" she snapped.

"If I'd been a traitor, I'd have told you I'd fight with you, then gone over and fought with them," McQuaid retorted. "I told you I wouldn't help either one. And I didn't."

Rocky looked like a boiling volcano, but she didn't say another word. Bonnie had stopped halfway across the clearing, her eyes on Rocky. She was angry because he hadn't come last night. Seeing Rocky did little to soothe her feelings.

Rocky had switched her angry gaze to Bonnie. McQuaid wondered what was going to happen now. Looking at the two girls, he thought he had never seen two prettier or angrier young women in his life. Neither was making any effort to look pretty. Their beauty was something they couldn't help.

They were almost the same size, Rocky just a little more solid. But there the similarity ended. Bonnie had long red hair and blue eyes. Rocky's hair was black and done up in a tight bun, and her black eyes sparked fire.

"If you're not gone in ten seconds, I'm coming after you!" Rocky shouted.

McQuaid tensed. Bonnie had her gun with her. Rocky

didn't. Yet he knew that Rocky would go after her cousin if Bonnie held her ground. What would he do if Bonnie pulled her gun?

But Bonnie glared at Rocky a moment, then wheeled her horse around and put him to a gallop out of the clearing.

Rocky turned her angry eyes on McQuaid.

"Why weren't you man enough to tell us who you were?"

"I was trying to stay alive. You were the one who insisted I was going to help you in the fight. I told you I wouldn't."

"You'd better get out of this valley fast," Rocky said. "The next time anybody from the Hatchet sees you, he'll be shooting."

Rocky started to yank her horse around, but McQuaid stopped her. "You won't be shooting if you don't have your guns." He emptied the bullets out of both guns, then handed them to her. "By the time you get them loaded again, I'm hoping you'll be cooled off."

She pocketed the bullets and put the rifle in its boot and the revolver in its holster. "Don't count on it," she said and kicked her horse into a run down through the trees.

It was an hour before Cliff Usta rode into the clearing to demand an explanation for McQuaid's failure to show up for the fight.

"I'm staying out of this fight," McQuaid said.

"You hired on to help the Long Bow!" Usta snapped.

"You promised me some land you didn't even own. I'm being just as fair with you as you were with me."

Usta's face clouded angrily. "You won't ever own this land. It's Long Bow land and it's going to stay that way! You can leave on your horse or feet first. Your choice."

"I'm staying right here, feet down and head up,"

McQuaid said. "If you want to argue about that, now's a good time."

Usta glared at him but made no move for his gun. He just rode back the way he'd come.

McQuaid considered starting work on his cabin, but he knew it would be wasted effort. Someone would burn anything he built. And he'd make a perfect target for a bushwhacker while he was working on the place.

It was midafternoon when a big man rode boldly up the valley, passing by Patzel's Hatchet Ranch and coming to the clearing near the mouth of Hatchet Creek. He wasn't so tall, but he was fat. He slopped over the saddle like a sack of grain. As he reined up close to McQuaid, he grabbed the saddle horn and heaved himself twice before gathering enough momentum to roll his huge bulk over the cantle to the ground.

"I'm Sheriff Herb Ault," the man said. "George Yount came in late last night with the report that his freighter, Jim Ivy, was shot yesterday. He's sure someone on one of these ranches shot him."

McQuaid studied the fat man. He'd heard in Pinedale about Sheriff Ault. He hadn't been elected. The elected sheriff had moved away and the commissioners had appointed Ault to finish out the term. McQuaid had heard little good about the fat man.

"Why come to me about that?" McQuaid asked.

"You're Dan McQuaid, ain't you? I was told you were camped at the mouth of Hatchet Canyon. You've got quite a reputation. If I just ride into those ranches down there, I ain't going to get any answers. But if you're along, I figure I will."

"I'm no deputy."

"I can make you one if that's what's worrying you. I figure I'll find my man down there at the Hatchet. Ivy was killed on this side of the river."

"If you were killing someone, would you do it in your own yard?"

Ault frowned, a massive movement of heavy skin. "Don't figure this killing was planned. But it's murder just the same. If you don't come with me, I can use that as grounds for suspicion of murder and drag you in for that killing."

McQuaid wondered if that wasn't what Ault really had in mind, anyway. This might just be a ruse to get him to go with him peaceably.

"It'll take somebody bigger than you to take me in for a murder I hadn't heard of before," Dan said. "But I'll ride along with you if you want me to. I'd like to see how you stack up against fellows like Gideon and Walsh."

"That's what I'm taking you along for," Ault said.

"If you think I'm going to do your fighting for you, think again. I'm just going to watch."

Ault chewed his under lip. "They ain't going to know that. And you'd better not tell them. Come on."

McQuaid saddled his horse and rode down the valley with the sheriff to Patzel's Hatchet Ranch. He thought it might have been Ed Gideon who had killed the freighter. He'd come up the valley yesterday afternoon almost to McQuaid's clearing. He could have been coming from that killing.

McQuaid knew that he was in more danger than anybody Ault was planning to arrest. But he should be safe riding with the sheriff. Still, he kept his hand close to his gun and his eyes alert.

XII

Rocky was in the yard when McQuaid and the sheriff rode up. Neither Gideon nor Lintz were in sight. McQuaid had hoped that Gideon would be there. He wanted to see how Ed would react to the sheriff.

"You're not welcome here," Rocky snapped, her eyes on McQuaid.

"He ain't here because he wanted to come," Ault said. "I brought him. Jim Ivy was killed between here and town near that pile of rocks. Figured somebody here might know something about it."

"You mean the kid who hauls freight to Yount's store?" Rocky asked.

"Same one. George Yount was the one who told me."

"Are you accusing us?" Rocky's anger was turning on Ault now.

"I ain't accusing nobody yet. I'm just looking around and asking questions. Where's your old man?"

"Inside in bed," Rocky said. "Crippled."

Ault stared at Rocky and apparently decided not to pursue that further. "Where's your crew?"

"Out working," Rocky said. "This is a working ranch, you know."

"Don't get too high and mighty, miss," Ault wheezed. "I intend to find out who killed Ivy. I'm going over and talk to the Ustas. When I come back, you'd better have your crew here so I can talk to them."

103

Ault turned his horse around and headed for the creek. McQuaid followed. He could see that Rocky didn't know anything about the murder. She wasn't going out and bring in her crew so Ault could question them, either. From the way she took charge when Ault appeared, McQuaid was sure that she had assumed command of the Hatchet. It would likely be run better now than when Frank Patzel was in charge.

Their welcome at the Long Bow was as chilly as it had been at the Hatchet. Ault stated his case and demanded to talk to each one of the family and crew. Usta curtly informed him he could talk to those that were there. He offered no explanation as to where the others were and made it clear that he had no intention of sending for them. Toby Walsh was among those missing.

Ault concentrated on questioning Kenny Coy, the foreman. He knew nothing about Ivy's murder and hadn't even heard about it till Ault told him. McQuaid believed him. He wondered what Walsh would have said if he'd been here. Ault likely wouldn't have questioned him very closely. McQuaid didn't take Ault for a man anxious to tangle with a fast gun.

"You ain't exactly needed up here," Usta said when Ault finished talking to Coy.

"I'm going to find out who killed Jim Ivy," Ault said. "I hear there's been a lot of bickering up here, too. I'm going to put a deputy in Arrow with authority to drag in anybody who starts a fight. Is that clear?"

"Clear as a muddy creek," Cliff Usta grunted. "Just keep your deputy in Arrow. He'll be safe there."

Ault swelled up even bigger, but he didn't put his anger into words. He moved out of the yard and headed back across the creek. Usta was glaring at McQuaid more than Ault as they left.

"Didn't find out much there," McQuaid commented as they rode out of the creek on the south side.

"Oh, I think we did," Ault said. "Nobody over on the Usta side knows anything about the murder. It has to be one of the Patzels."

"Which one?" McQuaid asked, failing to follow the sheriff's reasoning.

"I don't know yet," Ault said, eyes squinted in thought. "But I'll find out. Thanks for riding with me, McQuaid."

McQuaid nodded and reined up his horse. He'd been dismissed, but something about the sheriff struck a suspicious spark in his mind. Suddenly it hit him. Ault had been calling him McQuaid. How did he know his name was McQuaid? McQuaid had told everybody except the Ustas that his name was Quill.

McQuaid rode on to the trees that fringed the valley. There he turned east instead of west. Staying out of sight in the trees, he watched the sheriff. Ault rode into the Hatchet yard but didn't stay long. Heading east on the road that bent around the curve toward Arrow, he rode with his eyes on the ground. A short distance from the ranch, he reined to the south into the trees ahead of McQuaid.

McQuaid stopped. What was the sheriff up to? Curiosity and an uneasy feeling he couldn't identify made McQuaid push ahead.

He moved slowly as he neared the place where Ault had come into the trees. Then he saw him up ahead. Ault was off his horse talking to Rocky, who was also dismounted. McQuaid reined up and watched. This was none of his business, but he hadn't liked the way Ault had threatened Rocky when they'd been at the Hatchet. Deep down, he didn't like Herb Ault and he didn't trust him.

Suddenly he saw Ault pull his gun and aim it at Rocky. She didn't flinch and McQuaid was too far away to hear what she was saying. Dismounting, he tied his horse and moved forward silently to get within hearing range.

"You're going to tell me where your hired hands are, all right," Ault said. "If you don't, I'm going to arrest you for killing Ivy. If you didn't do it, you're at least harboring the criminal."

"You brainless tub of lard!" Rocky stormed. "You know I don't know anything about it."

"Careful with your names," Ault warned. He looked around, then back at Rocky. "I'm going to throw you in jail and lose the key." He grinned. "I might come and visit you once in a while so you won't get lonesome."

She swung a fist at him then, as he grabbed the gun out of her holster. She didn't scream, but McQuaid could see that she had allowed herself to get into a helpless position. Apparently she hadn't thought of Ault, who wore the sheriff's star, as being an enemy and she had allowed him to get close enough to disarm her.

Rocky put up a good fight. Ault wasn't particularly strong, McQuaid thought, but there was so much of him that he simply enveloped Rocky and smothered her punches.

"Calm down now, you spitfire!" Ault puffed. "You had your chance to help me. Now I'll get whatever I want, including a confession to that murder."

If Rocky made a reply, it was smothered in those rolls of fat because Ault had Rocky squeezed up against him where she couldn't swing her fists.

McQuaid had heard and seen enough. He had never fought a law officer, but there was a first time for everything. He moved forward silently. Ault and Rocky were making far more noise than McQuaid was so he had no fear of being detected.

The hulking sheriff swung around when McQuaid was still ten feet away. His little eyes widened behind their rolls of fat and he pushed Rocky away from him. He reached for the gun in his holster, but McQuaid was close enough to get to him before he could get it clear.

He smashed his right fist into Ault's face while his left hand grabbed the sheriff's right arm. Jerking Ault's hand back, he flipped the gun out of his fingers.

Ault roared like a wounded bull and charged forward. McQuaid sidestepped. He wasn't afraid to exchange blows with the sheriff, but he didn't want to try to stop the momentum of all that bulk. As Ault went past, he hammered a hard fist into his face, smearing blood over his fat nose and mouth.

The sheriff got stopped, like a freight train coming to a halt, and turned back. McQuaid was there and he began hammering the sheriff around the face and neck. Ault didn't try to charge again. Throwing up his hands to defend his face, he began to retreat. McQuaid didn't let him get out of range or catch his breath. Ault was puffing like an engine pulling twenty loaded cars upgrade. Since Ault was protecting his head with both arms, McQuaid lowered his aim and drove a fist with all his force into that flabby yielding belly. Air exploded out of the sheriff's lungs and he sat down with a grunt, his arms dropping helplessly into his lap.

McQuaid backed up to Rocky and found her unhurt but seething with fury. Seeing that McQuaid had backed off, Ault clambered to his feet and headed for his horse. Only when he was mounted did he turn back to McQuaid.

"I'll be back, McQuaid. And I'm going to drag you into jail and let you rot there!"

"Why not take me in now?" McQuaid asked.

Ault swore and kicked his horse into a slow gallop down the creek bank. McQuaid turned to find Rocky studying him as if he were a stranger.

"I don't like being beholden to anybody," she said. "But I am to you. Ault will get you now if he can. You'd better stay on the Hatchet tonight."

"You might be right," he said, marveling at the change

in her. She had been ready to kill him on sight earlier today. Now she was offering him sanctuary from a sheriff with a seriously damaged pride. "You can ask Gideon about Ivy's murder," he went on. "He was gunning for me yesterday afternoon. Must have been soon after Ivy was killed. And he came from down the valley."

She nodded, watching him closely. He doubted if she had heard a word he'd said. "You didn't have any call to help me. Why did you?"

"I usually do what I want to," he said, realizing he hadn't thought about his reasons, either. "That's what I did then."

She let it drop, but he could see that she was still puzzled. He could do some thinking on that himself. If he'd let Ault take Rocky away, he wouldn't have had any worries about her threats. And those threats had not been idle ones. Maybe they were canceled now; she was offering him sanctuary.

Rocky had some explaining to do at the Hatchet when she brought McQuaid in. But when she made it an order that McQuaid was to be treated like one of the crew, the objections subsided. McQuaid resolved to get away from the Hatchet tomorrow. Rocky didn't enjoy explaining his presence here.

Ollie Heinze and Willy Lintz didn't question Rocky's orders. But Ed Gideon had plenty to say in the bunkhouse. Heinze exploded. If Gideon didn't like Rocky's orders, he could pack up and get off the Hatchet. Gideon shut up and McQuaid guessed why. Gideon's and Walsh's plot, if there was one, couldn't be carried out if he left.

McQuaid lay awake on his bunk long after the lights were put out. When he saw Gideon slip out of his bunk and through the door, he eased his feet to the floor and got into his clothes and followed.

He lost some time getting dressed and buckling on his gun. He wasn't going to follow Gideon without his weapon. He checked the corral, but the horses were all there. That must mean that wherever Gideon was going was within walking distance.

Each night as the moon approached its fullest stage, it shone brighter and longer before setting behind the mountains to the west. There was enough light for McQuaid to see fairly well. He found boot marks going down the trail where only horses went during the day. He followed cautiously.

Less than two hundred yards from the bunkhouse, the tracks turned off the trail toward the trees along the south canyon wall. McQuaid knew he was taking a big chance crossing that open moonlit meadow toward the trees. But that was where Gideon had gone. He followed.

He reached the trees without challenge. Probably Gideon had gone far enough back into the trees that he couldn't see the meadow. McQuaid worked his way through the trees, careful not to make any noise.

The sound of voices caught his ear and he moved silently toward them. He stopped when he saw Gideon in a small clearing with Walsh. McQuaid was close enough now to hear what they were saying. Walsh was angry because Willy Lintz wasn't there.

"Willy and I agreed that he'd stay in the bunkhouse," Gideon said sharply. "One of us slipping out without McQuaid seeing was risk enough."

"Are you sure he didn't see you?"

"I'm sure," Gideon said. "I listened outside the bunkhouse and I didn't hear a sound inside. McQuaid was asleep."

"You should have knifed him in his sleep. We have to get rid of him."

"If anything happens to McQuaid while he's on the Hatchet, they'll know I did it. If I get in trouble, our whole plan goes up in smoke."

"I reckon," Walsh muttered. "I wish I had a chance

like that. I wouldn't care what anybody thought. I'd kill him. Do you think Willy will do his part when we're ready?"

"I don't know," Gideon admitted. "But he knows too much to cut him out now. Besides, we need him."

"If Niccum was here, we wouldn't have to depend on the likes of Willy." Walsh paced across the tiny clearing and back. "Having McQuaid right under your nose isn't going to help us. What got into Rocky to bring him there?"

"Ault was trying to make off with Rocky, the way I hear it. McQuaid stepped in and pounded him up. Rocky was grateful. That won't change any of our plans, will it?"

"Don't see why it should. Doesn't look like the ranches are going to fight another battle soon."

"Does that mean we go ahead with our plan involving Rocky and Bonnie?"

"Right," Walsh said. "But we better get rid of McQuaid first. While he's right there on the Hatchet, can't you make something happen that will look like an accident? Ambush him if you have to and make them think I did it. I don't care. Just get rid of him!"

McQuaid could see that the conference was about over. He backed off silently. Twenty yards away, he stepped on a stick that snapped like a pistol shot.

Walsh's gun popped into his hand and he touched Gideon's arm. "If that's McQuaid, we've got to get him," he said just loudly enough for McQuaid to hear. "But don't crowd your luck. He can shoot straight."

McQuaid eased backward again. He could force a showdown now, but he didn't like the odds of two against one and they knew this area better than he did. He retreated to the west, thinking he might go back to Hatchet Creek for the night. But when he stopped to listen, he heard nothing. Maybe neither Walsh nor Gideon was too eager to press his luck. Or possibly they had decided some animal had made that noise.

Following the trees to the place where they came closest to the Hatchet buildings, McQuaid finally left them and scurried across to the bunkhouse and to bed. Gideon was not back yet so McQuaid snuggled down as though he had not been gone.

McQuaid didn't sleep. He wanted to watch Gideon when he came in. Gideon might decide to use his knife. But he didn't come. McQuaid wondered if he had left too soon. Maybe the two had more planning to do. He heard some racket outside and expected Gideon to open the door and enter. But he didn't.

Then suddenly McQuaid was brought wide awake by the smell of smoke. Before his feet hit the floor, he heard the crackle of flames. The fire was erupting in the wall right beside his bed, and it was shooting up rapidly in the dry wood.

"Fire!" he yelled and both Heinze and Willy hit the floor.

"Get water from the tank!" Heinze shouted.

McQuaid made a dash for the door without even grabbing his clothes. He slammed against the door, but it didn't budge. It was blocked shut.

XIII

McQuaid turned toward Heinze. "We're locked in."

"Must be the Ustas," Heinze yelled. "They're trying to roast us alive!"

"How'll we get out?" Willy Lintz wailed.

"Grab your boots and pants!" Heinze shouted. "We'll break out the window!"

McQuaid doubted if it was the Ustas who had set this fire. He was guessing that it was Ed Gideon. Gideon and Walsh had agreed that he must be killed. A fire was a perfect way. The fact that Willy and Heinze would die, too, would not hinder Gideon.

Heinze had grabbed a stool from beside his bunk and had jammed the legs through the glass of the front window. It wasn't a big window, but it would be big enough for them to crawl through if all the glass could be pushed out.

"Better have your gun in one hand and your boots and pants in the other," Heinze warned. "If the Long Bow's out there, they'll try to pick us off as we come out."

"I don't figure this is the Long Bow's doing," McQuaid said. "I'll go out first and see."

McQuaid had put on his pants. Now he grabbed his boots and gun. As quickly as possible, he pulled himself through the small window. There were no shots as he hit the ground. He jerked on his boots while Heinze was coming out. By the time Willy had made it, McQuaid and Heinze were carrying buckets toward the water tank.

Rocky and her mother joined in the bucket brigade. The fire had been started against the wall of the bunkhouse right outside McQuaid's bunk. McQuaid was betting that Gideon had hoped he would be overcome by smoke before he got out of his bunk.

Since McQuaid had discovered the fire early, it hadn't gotten much of a start. The water they threw on it soon put it out. The wall was charred and in one place burned through. But it could be patched up and would still be about as good as it originally was.

When the last wisp of smoke was gone, Rocky stood back and surveyed the damage. "That doesn't look like anything the Ustas would do," she said. She turned a sharp look at McQuaid. "What do you know about it?"

He wasn't surprised at her suspicions, but apparently Heinze was.

"It sure wasn't McQuaid who did it," he said emphatically. "Only a fool would start a fire when he was inside. Besides, he couldn't have blocked that door from the inside."

Rocky nodded. "Where's Ed?"

"He stepped outside and didn't come back," Heinze said, suspicion blooming in his round face.

"I still think you ought to ask him what he knows about Ivy's murder," McQuaid said. "I'll go back to Hatchet Creek tomorrow. I don't want to bring any more trouble on you here."

"You're not bringing trouble," Heinze objected.

"I think that fire was set for my benefit," McQuaid said.

"You can stay," Rocky said.

Heinze and McQuaid moved the two big logs away from the door and opened it. The inside of the bunkhouse smelled of smoke, so they left the door open to air it out, while Willy went back in.

McQuaid went over to Willy Lintz's bunk before Heinze came in. "What do you know about the scheme Gideon and Walsh are cooking up?" he asked.

Willy's jaw dropped and his eyes widened in fear. "What scheme?" he whispered. "I don't know nothing about any scheme."

"You're supposed to be in on it," McQuaid said. "Are you?"

"I—I ain't in on nothing," Willy said.

McQuaid could see that Willy was too scared to talk. Walsh or Gideon would kill him if he spilled a word. But now that he realized his secret partnership with the two gunmen was known, maybe he'd consider his future actions a little more carefully.

After breakfast the next morning, McQuaid got his horse. He couldn't see how he could help any here and he would surely bring more trouble. Rocky had enough trouble. Her father was in bed, nursing his wound, and her mother spent most of her time with him. That sort of left Rocky in charge.

She still didn't fully trust him. That was obvious from her suspicions concerning the fire. She had repaid him for helping her yesterday by letting him spend the night on the Hatchet.

As he rode up the valley toward Hatchet Creek, he was alert. He was the prime target of both Ed Gideon and Toby Walsh. Rocky had calmed down from her fury at discovering that he was really Dan McQuaid. But Cliff Usta wasn't appeased yet. He'd welcome the news of McQuaid's death.

McQuaid didn't worry about facing Usta in a fight. That wasn't Usta's way. He'd find someone else to do his dangerous jobs for him. Walsh worked for Usta and he wanted McQuaid dead, anyway. So Walsh was the man McQuaid had to watch for.

The best way to defend himself against an attack from Walsh was to go after the gunman and force the battle on his own terms. If he didn't, Walsh would pick a time and place to his advantage.

Reaching the trees, Dan rode past the high knoll where he hoped to build his cabin. He still wanted to stay out of the war between the Ustas and Patzels. But he found himself favoring the Patzels now. Maybe it was because they were the underdogs with Frank Patzel out of action. The Hatchet had fewer men and two of them were in a scheme to overthrow both ranches. But there was another element now that he had to admit to himself. Rocky was getting to him.

McQuaid crossed Hatchet Creek, then turned across Long Bow Creek and went into the trees along the north wall. Turning back east, he rode as close to the Long Bow as he could. Although he watched until well past noon, he saw no sign of Toby Walsh. Walsh should have been at the ranch for dinner, at least.

In the early afternoon, Cliff Usta came out, saddled a horse, and rode slowly up the valley. McQuaid wondered where he was going, but when he turned toward Hatchet Creek, he guessed Cliff might be going up to see him.

McQuaid mounted and rode west, then cut down toward Hatchet Creek himself. He had no fear of facing Cliff Usta alone.

He came within sight of Usta before Usta was halfway up Hatchet Creek to the knoll where McQuaid camped. The Long Bow owner was concentrating on what lay ahead and McQuaid was close before he heard him. Usta jumped as if shot when he saw McQuaid. But his hand stayed away from his gun.

"Any special reason for coming to see me?" McQuaid asked.

"Just wanted to give you a last chance to change your mind and help us move the Patzels out of the valley," Usta said.

"Thought maybe you got enough fighting the other night."

"We didn't," Usta said. "I think maybe they did. Now is the time to finish it. Frank's out of it for a while. It'll be easy. You can't earn the right to stay here on this land any easier than that."

"You don't have that right to give. Remember?" McQuaid leaned over the horn of his saddle. "Mr. Usta, have you considered the possibility that Toby Walsh is double-crossing you?"

Usta stared at McQuaid. "Of course not. Walsh is a good man."

"You'd better check on that before you trust him too far."

"I trust him," Usta said. "What about you coming to help us?"

"If you're too bullheaded to see what Walsh is doing, I reckon I'd be a fool to trust you an inch."

Usta scowled. "I should have known it was a waste of time riding up here to see you. We'll get rid of the Hatchet Ranch on our own. And when we do, you'd better be out of this valley. You won't live here, I promise."

Usta wheeled his horse around and rode back down Hatchet Creek toward Long Bow Creek. McQuaid watched him, knowing that Usta had been showing his true colors when he said that he wouldn't let McQuaid live here.

But McQuaid had been threatened before. His biggest danger was still Toby Walsh. Ed Gideon came second and Usta ran a poor third. He thought of that meeting between Gideon and Walsh not far from the Hatchet last night. He remembered what Gideon had said about the plans for Rocky and Bonnie. Walsh had agreed that the plans were unchanged. But neither one had said what they were. It sounded ominous to McQuaid and gave him an additional reason for getting to Walsh before he had time to create more mischief.

He rode into Hatchet Canyon and selected the spot where he would spend the night near the place where he'd been a couple of nights ago. He had to make sure that he had a place he could defend and one where he wouldn't be easily surprised.

He was coming out of the canyon when he heard a horse plunging up Hatchet Creek. That horse was being run hard with no consideration for silence.

McQuaid turned his horse toward the knoll, sure that whoever was coming wanted to see him and would come there. He was astonished, however, when he saw the rider, Morton Usta.

McQuaid felt that Morton Usta had been partly responsible for the beating he'd gotten in Arrow at the dance. He didn't trust Morton any more than he did Cliff Usta.

When Morton saw McQuaid, he pulled his horse to a halt.

"What's chasing you?" McQuaid asked. "You'll kill that horse."

"They'll kill me first," Morton said, fear cracking his voice.

"Who will?"

"Toby and Gideon," Morton said. "I stumbled onto them and they were talking about wiping out the Ustas and the Patzels so they could own the whole valley."

McQuaid nodded. "Did they see you?"

Morton bobbed his head. "They tried to kill me. They're going to kill all the Ustas."

"That hardly seems likely," McQuaid said, trying to calm Morton down. As tall as he was, it was hard to realize he was only seventeen years old. A lot of the boy was showing in him now.

"I heard them," Morton said, his voice almost a

scream. "And they tried to kill me! They're afraid I'll tell everybody what I heard."

"Have you?"

"I haven't seen anybody. I came right here. You're the only man in this whole valley that Toby is afraid of. If I'm with you, I'll be safe."

"I wouldn't bank on that," McQuaid said. "Walsh is after me, too."

"But he's scared of you," Morton babbled. "He ain't scared of nobody else."

"Are they after you now?"

"I think I gave them the slip," Morton said. "But I ain't sure. If they find me, they'll kill me."

"Are you helpless? Can't you use a gun?"

"Not against Toby or Gideon. They're too good for me."

"Could be," McQuaid admitted. "What did you hear them say?"

"Just what I told you. That they're going to wipe out both us and the Patzels and take over the whole valley."

"Did they say anything about Bonnie and Rocky?"

"I didn't hear anything about them. But I reckon they figure on killing them, too. They're going to kill us all."

"Why didn't you go tell your father?"

"Pa can't keep them away from me. You can."

McQuaid shook his head. "Not likely. Your pa will know what they're liable to do. You tell him, then stick close to him."

"Can't I stay with you?"

"I'm going down and warn the Patzels. Do you want to go down there?"

Morton shook his head. "Rocky would kill me sure if I set foot in their yard."

"You got up here all right. You can surely make it back home. I told your pa that Walsh was double-crossing him. He wouldn't believe me. Maybe he'll believe you.

If you don't warn him, Walsh will kill him, too."

Morton nodded vigorously and reined his horse around riding down the trail as if he had a band of Indians after him.

McQuaid turned his horse toward the Hatchet Ranch. As he neared the buildings, he rode more cautiously, watching the corrals and bunkhouse. Gideon might be desperate enough to shoot at him regardless of the consequences. If he and Walsh knew that Morton Usta was wise to their scheme, they might make a desperate attempt to wipe out both families before they were warned.

Seeing Rocky come out of the house, McQuaid headed for the yard gate. Ollie Heinze came from the corral to wait for him. Dan didn't see either Willy or Gideon.

"You didn't stay long," Rocky said. "Decide that you liked it here?"

"I just had a visitor, Morton Usta. He's running as scared as anybody I've ever seen. He stumbled onto Ed Gideon and Toby Walsh plotting to kill all the Usta and Patzel families and take over the whole valley."

"I can't believe that," Rocky said.

"I've seen scared men before," McQuaid said. "When they're as scared as young Usta was, they don't lie. Besides, I've seen Gideon and Walsh together myself. They're up to something. Morton Usta heard them making plans."

"Got any idea when they'll try it?" Heinze asked. "Or how they're going to go about it?"

McQuaid shook his head. "Young Usta didn't hear any details. They chased him but he got away. I sent him back to warn his family. I'd say your best bet is to forget this feud and band together to fight Walsh and Gideon."

Rocky shook her head. "There's no way Uncle Cliff and us are going to fight on the same side."

"You might die apart then," McQuaid said angrily. "Think about it."

Wheeling around, he rode back to Hatchet Canyon

where he spent the night in the little nook he had picked out.

By midmorning the next day, he was back at the Hatchet to see what Rocky had done. She was just as stubborn as ever and their quarrel picked up where it had dropped the day before.

A rider coming up the valley took their attention then and McQuaid watched him closely. He hadn't seen the man before. He glanced at Rocky and Heinze and saw the puzzled looks on their faces. As the man got closer, McQuaid saw the deputy sheriff's star on his vest. This must be the deputy that Ault said he was going to put at Arrow. Rocky had seen the star, too, and her face grew tense and her hand rested on her gun.

The rider reined up close to them. He was small and sat his saddle easily. He had a sharp nose and light brown hair. But it was his eyes that caught McQuaid's attention. They were light blue, so light that they appeared almost colorless.

"I'm the new deputy sheriff down at Arrow," the man said in a nasal tone. He looked from one to the other. "I take it this is the Hatchet Ranch." His eyes traveled on to McQuaid. "You must be McQuaid."

McQuaid nodded. The man had his left side to the three of them. Suddenly his right hand came up over his thighs with a gun pointed at McQuaid.

"I'm taking you in," he said.

XIV

McQuaid stared at the deputy. His move to get his gun in his hand had been pretty clever. McQuaid hadn't seen it.

"Just what is the charge?" he asked.

"Murder. You killed Morton Usta yesterday."

McQuaid scowled. "I did not."

"You don't deny you were with him, do you?"

"How would you prove I was if I said I wasn't?" McQuaid asked, wondering where he was getting his information.

"A man named Walsh saw you with him up close to a place called Hatchet Creek. Then a few minutes later you shot him. That was on Hatchet Creek, too."

"Walsh? That figures. Morton said he was afraid Walsh would kill him."

"Just unbuckle your gun belt real easy, McQuaid," the deputy said.

"When did Ault put you up here at Arrow?"

"I got there last night if it's any of your business. My name's Vinny Niccum."

McQuaid nodded. That tied the knot in the mule's tail. Walsh and Gideon had been talking about how the odds would be in their favor when Niccum got here. But McQuaid hadn't expected Niccum to be wearing a lawman's star. If Niccum was Ault's deputy, he wondered if Ault himself might not be in on Walsh's scheme. If so, the odds were heavily in favor of Walsh and his companions now. Niccum appeared to be a slick hand with a gun. Walsh was good and Gideon claimed to be. Only Ault among those four failed to measure up as a gunman.

McQuaid carefully unbuckled his gun belt and let it drop. That gun in Niccum's hand was very steady. If Niccum was with Walsh in this, he'd like nothing better than an excuse to shoot him.

"You're making a bad mistake," Rocky said, frowning at the proceedings. "McQuaid hasn't killed anybody."

"Don't stuff me with lies, miss," Niccum said. "McQuaid's reputation is known everywhere west of the Missouri. Killing a kid like Morton Usta would be nothing to him. But he's going to pay for it this time."

"Did I shoot him in the front or back?" McQuaid asked.

"Makes no difference. He wasn't any gunfighter. You are. Now turn your horse around slow. I want to get at that rifle."

McQuaid obeyed, weighing his chances of making a break and knowing they were next to nothing.

"I don't believe he did it, either," Heinze put in.

"I don't care what you believe, mister," Niccum said. "I've got a witness who says McQuaid was with Morton just before he was killed and the boy's father says that McQuaid had threatened them because they didn't want him up on that land. That's plenty of reason to take him in."

"You don't have any place to put him in Arrow," Rocky said. "Arrow's never had a jail."

"Pinedale does," Niccum said. "That's where he's going." He reached over and slipped the rifle out of its boot. "Now get your hands up above your head while I get down."

McQuaid obeyed, watching Niccum slip out of the saddle to the ground like a stalking cat. He kept his gun pointed at McQuaid every instant while he picked up McQuaid's gun. Then he flipped open a saddlebag and took out some ropes. He tossed these to Heinze.

"Tie him up, mister. And you'd better do a good job or I might just drag you in as an accomplice."

Heinze frowned. "I didn't kill nobody although I might've had more reason for doing it than McQuaid did." Then he took the ropes Niccum had tossed to him and tied McQuaid's hands to the saddle horn. Next, at Niccum's direction, he tied McQuaid's feet together under the horse's belly.

"At least you won't fall off," Niccum said as Heinze backed away. Niccum tested the ropes binding McQuaid's hands. Satisfied, he got back on his horse and gave the order to move, and McQuaid kneed his horse onto the trail leading down the valley toward Arrow.

McQuaid refused to let his horse be hurried. He knew that Niccum was Walsh's man, so he was sure that he would never get to Arrow. Somewhere between here and Arrow, Walsh would show up. Then Walsh would get to do what he'd been wanting to do all the time—kill McQuaid. Looking back, he saw that both Heinze and Rocky had disappeared.

"Where are you going to meet Walsh?" McQuaid asked, finally breaking the silence.

"I ain't meeting Walsh or anybody," Niccum said, startled. "I can get you to jail by myself."

"Is Ault in this with you and Walsh?"

Niccum swore. "Shut your mouth I was sent up here to arrest you for killing young Usta. That's all."

The more McQuaid thought of it, the more it seemed likely that Ault was in with Walsh and Gideon. If he wasn't, it was a streak of pure luck that Niccum should get the job of deputy sheriff and then be stationed at Arrow just when Walsh and Gideon needed him.

It was over four miles from the Hatchet Ranch to Arrow. McQuaid tried to guess where Walsh would show up. And he tried desperately to think of some way to thwart the plan that he was sure had been made. When Walsh showed up, it would be too late to do anything.

Niccum kept turning in his saddle and looking back and finally, after they had begun the big swing to the south as the valley ran down to the big canyon beyond Arrow, Niccum motioned toward the trees.

"We're sitting ducks out here in this open valley," he said. "We'll be safer out of sight."

"Who are you afraid of?" McQuaid asked. "That foreman wouldn't hurt a flea. Maybe it's Rocky. Are you afraid of girls, Niccum?"

"Shut up!" Niccum snapped. "I take care of my prisoners."

"I'll bet you do," McQuaid said softly.

He had no choice but to go where Niccum guided his horse and they were soon in the trees, hidden from the valley. It didn't surprise McQuaid, when they started across a small glen, to see Toby Walsh waiting on his horse at the far edge of the clearing.

McQuaid's mind raced, looking for any means of escape. There was none. Walsh had his gun in his hand, aimed at McQuaid.

Niccum reined up and stopped McQuaid's horse. Walsh rode slowly across the clearing. His eyes were shining like black beads in the rain as they focused on McQuaid.

"I knew someday I'd catch you," Walsh said. "Now you'll learn to keep your nose out of business that don't concern you."

"He's my prisoner," Niccum said weakly.

"Not anymore," Walsh said, not moving his gun or his eyes from McQuaid. "He killed Morton. I'm making sure some court don't turn him loose."

McQuaid glanced at Niccum. He was sitting quietly on his horse, not making any move. If there had been any doubt in McQuaid's mind that this was a setup, it was gone now.

"You've got the drop on me," Niccum said. "Ain't much I can do."

"That's sure," Walsh agreed. "They'll find McQuaid out here in a day or two." He held up a broken rowelled spur. "This is Cliff Usta's. Everybody knows it's his. When they find this next to McQuaid, they'll be sure that Cliff and Skip Usta killed him. They're telling everybody they see that they're going to get him for killing Morton."

Walsh and Niccum had planned it well. McQuaid could see no flaw in their reasoning. Now the law would take the Ustas out of Walsh's way. Frank Patzel was already crippled. They would soon have the valley to themselves.

Walsh motioned with his gun for McQuaid to nudge his horse toward the trees across the clearing. But at that moment, a rifle spanged and the top of the horn on Walsh's saddle disappeared.

Walsh wheeled toward the sound and another rifle bullet dug deeper into the saddle horn. The horse started bucking. Before Walsh had him quieted, Rocky appeared in the clearing, her rifle wavering between Walsh and Niccum. McQuaid didn't doubt that she could and would shoot either man if he made a move to turn a gun on her.

"Drop the gun, Toby," Rocky snapped. "Mister, you'd better just sit tight," she said to Niccum.

Walsh started to drop his gun, but then jerked it up. Rocky's rifle roared again and Walsh flinched as the bullet nicked his arm and drew blood.

Rocky cocked the rifle again. "Next time it'll be dead center. I promise."

Walsh let his gun fall to the ground. Rocky looked at Niccum, but he wasn't making any move toward his gun. His face was flushed with anger, though, as he glared at the girl.

"This will cost you a few years in prison," the deputy snarled. "You can't interfere with the law."

"Toby Walsh is not the law!" Rocky snapped.

"I am," Niccum said.

"Then why in blazes weren't you doing something about Walsh stealing your prisoner? You're as much a murderer as he is. You meant to kill McQuaid. I'm going to give you your chance in a few minutes. Bring your horse over here, McQuaid."

McQuaid nudged his horse into action, guiding him with his knees, careful not to get between Rocky and the two men. He kneed the horse around close to Rocky.

Without taking her rifle off the two men, she pulled a hunting knife from its sheath at her hip and slashed the rope on McQuaid's wrists. Then she handed him the knife and he leaned down, cutting the rope binding his feet under the horse's belly.

"Get down and limber up," she said to McQuaid. "Then take one of Walsh's guns. The one on the ground ought to do."

He saw then what Rocky had in mind. He wasn't sure that facing the two men on equal terms would be a good idea, but Rocky had freed him and was giving him a chance. He had no reason to object.

As soon as his fingers were limbered up, he walked over and picked up Walsh's gun, making sure he didn't get between Rocky and the men. He dropped the gun in his holster and got the feel of it. Very much like his own, which Niccum still had.

"Now then," Rocky said, "if you're so dead set on killing McQuaid, hop to it."

McQuaid watched the two. Walsh showed no inclination to accept Rocky's offer, although he still had one gun. Niccum looked as if he would accept the challenge. But when he saw Walsh back down, his enthusiasm died, too. McQuaid had the idea that Niccum might be even

better with a gun than Walsh. Walsh had practically said
as much that day to Gideon.

"No takers?" McQuaid asked.

"A lawman doesn't have to stoop to a gunfight to
uphold the law," Niccum growled.

"If you're not going to use those guns, shed them,"
McQuaid said. "All of them."

He watched as Walsh dropped his other gun and Niccum dropped his rifle and revolver and the gun he had
taken from McQuaid.

"When you're willing to tell the judge in Pinedale
exactly what happened here, I'll be glad to give your
guns back," McQuaid said.

McQuaid mounted his horse again after collecting the
hardware on the ground. Rocky still kept her rifle on the
two men. McQuaid and Rocky retreated to the edge of
the clearing. Walsh and Niccum sat their horses sullenly,
fury working in their faces.

"Move out," McQuaid ordered and watched Niccum
and Walsh disappear into the trees. Then he and Rocky
turned toward the Hatchet. "We'll have to watch them,"
he said as they put their horses to a gallop.

"Right now they're no threat. A rattlesnake with no
fangs can't do much," Rocky said.

"Thanks is pretty poor pay for what you just did for
me," McQuaid said.

"I don't want any thanks," Rocky said. "I work for
myself. I don't think you killed Morton Usta. Besides,
I need your gun in my camp."

"Lady, you've got it," McQuaid said, "even if it is
against my principles to get into this war. I was a dead
man back there till you stepped in. I owe you."

"Ollie and I should have thrown down on that deputy
when he first showed up. Why would the sheriff hire a
deputy like that?"

"I'm not sure he did," McQuaid said. "But if he did,

it means that Ault is in on the deal with Walsh and Gideon."

"You still think they're scheming against both ranches?"

McQuaid nodded. "That's what Morton Usta found out. It's why Walsh killed him. The way I hear it, Willy is supposed to be with them, too, but he's dragging his feet. If Ault has joined them, they've got more guns than either you or the Ustas now. Your only hope of whipping them is to join forces."

Rocky shook her head. "No chance of that. Uncle Cliff and Aunt Jane are determined to have this whole valley for themselves."

"If you could make them see that they either share it with you or give it all to Walsh and Gideon, they might change their minds."

Again Rocky shook her head. "Can't be done. We'll stand off Walsh if he comes after us. Then we'll send the Ustas packing. That's how it's going to be."

McQuaid shook his head. He'd seen some stubborn people but none to top Rocky Patzel. There were others like her on both ranches, too. That was why Walsh and Gideon had been able to work out this plan and make it go. Neither outfit would take its mind off the other long enough to see the danger sneaking up on its flanks.

It was after noon when they got back to the ranch. The noon meal had been held up till Rocky returned. Ed Gideon was not there again. He hadn't been on the ranch for more than a day now. Ollie Heinze was angry but still not totally convinced by McQuaid's story. Willy Lintz was there, but he wouldn't talk to anyone.

McQuaid again suggested the necessity of joining forces with the Long Bow. Both Alice and Frank Patzel vehemently objected. Frank was still in bed, but he was feeling well enough to join in the argument.

McQuaid tried to corner Willy Lintz after dinner to find out just where he stood, but he hurried off to check some cattle. Willy was scared. But was he afraid the

Patzels would find out about his double-cross, or was he afraid of Walsh and Gideon because he hadn't gone all out to help them?

It seemed to be a waiting game, not even Rocky having any concrete plan for action. Willy came in for supper, and he and Ollie Heinze and McQuaid went to the bunkhouse after the meal.

It was shortly after they got there that the raiders struck. They opened up with rifles.

Then the firing stopped and Cliff Usta yelled at the main house. "Send out that killer, McQuaid. He killed Morton and he's going to pay for it."

Trying to see through the darkness caused by clouds over the moon, McQuaid thought he recognized Toby Walsh standing near Usta. If Walsh had Niccum with him, the Hatchet was in real trouble.

XV

The bunkhouse had two windows, one close to the door and the other on the opposite side. Ollie Heinze took the window across from the door and assigned McQuaid to the door and Willy to the window next to it, the one Heinze had broken out to escape the fire a couple of nights ago. McQuaid guessed that Heinze was getting suspicious of Willy, too.

"Are you going to send him out?" Usta yelled.

"He didn't kill Morton," Rocky shouted back from the main house.

"Oh, yes, he did. I saw him." That was Walsh's voice.

So Walsh was out there, too. He must have convinced Cliff Usta that McQuaid had killed Morton, which probably hadn't been too hard. That kept suspicion away from Walsh and had probably triggered this raid against the Patzels. In the fighting, some of the men who stood between Walsh and control of the valley were likely to get killed.

McQuaid thought about Gideon, but he doubted if he was in on this raid. Cliff Usta wouldn't allow a Hatchet man to side with him. Vinny Niccum might be there, though.

"I know McQuaid is with your outfit," Usta shouted again. "We'll give you five minutes to send him out. Then we're coming after him."

McQuaid wished he could talk to Rocky, but she was over in the house and he was stuck here with Heinze and Willy in the bunkhouse.

"Do you think you're on the wrong side?" McQuaid asked Willy softly.

Willy Lintz shot a glance at Dan. "I shouldn't be in this fight at all," he said.

"Walsh is out there. Maybe Gideon, too."

Willy shook his head. "Ed ain't out there. That's the Long Bow outfit."

"Gideon isn't exactly fighting for the Hatchet," McQuaid said.

"He sure ain't fighting for the Long Bow."

"What do you think they'll do, Ollie?" McQuaid called across to Heinze.

"Pick us off if they can. If they can't do that, they'll try burning us out."

"Think they'll try to set fire to the house?"

"Could be," Ollie said. "When we start shooting, they're going to know that we're out here, and Rocky and her folks are alone in the house."

"Maybe I ought to go over there," McQuaid said.

"That won't be an easy trip."

"I think I can make it."

McQuaid figured the five minutes Usta had given Rocky to send him out were about up. If he was going to get across to the house, he'd better do it now. It would catch the raiders by surprise and he could be halfway across the empty space between the buildings before they were aware of what was going on.

"Can you handle things here?" McQuaid asked Heinze.

"Sure," Ollie said. "But I wouldn't give much for your chances of getting across to the house."

"I'll be depending on you and your rifle," McQuaid said.

The bunkhouse door was open a crack. He eased it halfway open. Ollie Heinze came across to the door.

"We'll cover you," Heinze said softly. "Willy, you be ready to shoot at anything out there that moves."

Willy crouched by the hole that had been a window. "I'll be ready," he promised.

McQuaid wondered how much he could depend on Willy. But Heinze would do all he could to protect him as he dodged toward the house.

Ducking low, he slipped out of the door. Then, bending down as far as he could and still run with speed, he headed for the house. He was halfway across the yard before a man yelled and then a rifle roared.

Immediately Ollie's rifle bellowed from the doorway of the bunkhouse and another rifle joined in from the kitchen window of the house. McQuaid dodged wildly as he aimed for the kitchen door. More rifles out by the barn and corrals and haystacks opened up, but the two rifles in the bunkhouse and one from the house answered with enough authority to keep anybody from exposing himself to take deliberate aim. McQuaid hit the door and fell into the house without collecting any unwanted lead.

"Why did you do that?" Rocky demanded as she slammed the door shut behind him.

"Ollie thinks they might try to burn the house. Didn't figure you could watch both the front and back."

Rocky nodded. "Ma is trying to watch the other half. But she won't leave Pa too long. He's worked up fit to be tied."

Nothing more was said about the five-minute deadline Usta had given Rocky. The shooting had started now and it didn't stop. Glass tinkled as bullets hit windows. McQuaid found himself a window and fired at every flash he saw. The positions of the flashes changed, testifying to the uncomfortable accuracy of the defenders' fire.

For a while, it seemed the rifles were getting closer. Then suddenly McQuaid was aware that the shots were coming from farther away.

"They're backing off," he said.

"Guess they realize they can't fight their way in," Rocky said.

McQuaid checked the other side of the house, finding Alice Patzel at one window, watching for any movement outside.

"They haven't showed up around here," she said.

"Let's hope they don't," McQuaid said and went back.

"They're starting a fire!" Rocky yelled in alarm.

McQuaid had seen the glow as soon as he came into the kitchen. As the blaze climbed upward, he saw that it was one of the haystacks beyond the corral. The smoke fringing the flame came toward the house. The wind was behind the fire, fanning it toward the barn, bunkhouse, and house. It would have to be put out.

McQuaid dropped down by the window and emptied his rifle in the direction of the attackers. They were at a disadvantage now because the fire, blazing rapidly in the dry hay, lit up the area where they were. McQuaid thought he might have nicked one of them.

The raiders ran for their horses and rode quickly back into the darkness. McQuaid couldn't be sure they were out of range, but he couldn't wait. They had to soak up the side of the barn next to that burning stack or it could catch fire. If it did, every building on the ranch would go.

Running to the bunkhouse, he was met by Heinze and Willy. Grabbing a bucket apiece and still carrying their rifles, they ran to the watering trough and filled the buckets.

McQuaid expected shots from the dark but none came. Rocky came out to stand guard while the three men carried water to douse the side of the barn. McQuaid grabbed a pitchfork and scraped all the hay away from the barn so that the fire couldn't eat its way along the ground from the stack to the barn.

Another haystack caught fire from the first one, but

it was farther away from the barn. One corner of the log corral was threatened by this but no buildings.

The blaze in the stacks died down. It would smolder for two or three days unless they soaked the ashes thoroughly. But the main threat to the buildings was over. McQuaid was surprised that the raiders had left.

"Better keep an eye open," he said. "Rocky, make sure your ma is watching. They might try to sneak back and set fire to the house."

The girl nodded. "What are you going to do?"

"Ollie and I will ride out and see if we can see where they went. Willy can carry more water to make sure all this fire is out."

The horses had stayed in the far side of the corral, away from the fire, and Heinze and McQuaid saddled up and rode to the east, the direction the raiders had gone.

They moved cautiously along the south side of the creek until McQuaid saw the place where the horses had crossed. Heinze dismounted and examined the grass and the mud along the edge of the creek.

"Went both ways," he announced, "but scattered on the way back like they were confused or didn't have a leader."

They rode back to the Hatchet, swinging to the south to make sure some of the raiders hadn't stayed behind in the trees. They came in to the corrals from the south. That's how McQuaid happened to see the man lying face down along the south side of an unburned haystack.

He swung over and dismounted. Heinze was beside him. Gingerly, they rolled the man over. Cliff Usta.

"Roll him back," Heinze whispered. "I'll bet he was shot in the back."

They rolled him back over and saw the two holes punched in the back of his shirt.

"It had to be one of them," McQuaid said. "Nobody

from the house or the bunkhouse could have hit him
here."

"Who would do that?" Heinze asked.

"Walsh," McQuaid said. "Or Niccum or Gideon. Niccum and Gideon don't belong to the Long Bow crew.
But one of them could have sneaked in and killed Usta
and nobody would have been the wiser."

Heinze nodded slowly. "Then you were really telling
the truth about Walsh and Gideon. This cuts down both
the leaders here in the valley. And Walsh and his pals
are one step closer to taking over."

"They must not have missed Cliff," McQuaid said,
"or they'd have taken him home."

They rode on to the house. As they swung down,
Heinze voiced his conclusions. "Rocky can run things
here. But who'll run the Long Bow? Maybe Mrs. Usta
will do it. She's a dead ringer for Mrs. Patzel."

Inside the house, they told Rocky and her parents what
they had found. Even Frank and Alice Patzel seemed
shaken by the news. There was no elation now that the
leader of the Long Bow was dead.

"I rode with him for years," Frank Patzel said in a
subdued tone. "We were friends till he got so greedy and
wanted all the valley for himself."

"We'd better put out guards," Rocky said. "They
might come back, especially when they find out Uncle
Cliff isn't with them."

McQuaid nodded. "I think that's a wise move. Ollie
and I will take turns."

"We'll use two at a time," Rocky said. "Ollie and I
will take one guard, Dan and Willy the other."

McQuaid didn't argue. It would be hard for one man
to watch for enemies in all directions.

Rocky and Ollie Heinze took the first guard and
McQuaid went to bed in the bunkhouse. It seemed only
a short time till he and Willy were roused and took their
places out beyond the buildings. Ollie had reported that

Skip Usta and Toby Walsh had come and taken Cliff
Usta's body away. Ollie hadn't challenged them.

"We'll ride all the way around the buildings," Mc-
Quaid suggested to Willy. "You go one way and I'll go
the other. We'll meet twice on every round. We won't
be so lonesome and it'll give us a good look at everything
that's going on."

Willy agreed and they started out riding slowly.
McQuaid had suggested this method of guarding the
ranch so he could keep an eye on Willy as well as the
buildings.

McQuaid had made two complete rounds of the buildings, meeting Willy twice on each round. Then he came
to their meeting place on the west side of the circle and
Willy wasn't there. Instead of riding on, McQuaid reined
up and waited. Willy ought to be here soon.

When he didn't show up in a couple of minutes,
McQuaid nudged his horse forward, pushing him to a
trot. He went half a circle and didn't see any sign of
Willy. He guessed what had happened. Either Willy had
gone off to report to Walsh and Gideon, or else he had
been kidnapped. Considering how scared the young
puncher had been all day, McQuaid guessed the latter.
In that case, they must have nabbed him as he was coming
around the south side of the buildings. McQuaid would
have been on the north side then.

Turning to the bunkhouse, McQuaid roused Ollie
Heinze and explained about Willy's disappearance and
what he thought had happened. Ollie said he'd stand
guard while McQuaid went looking for Willy.

"Walsh may have stayed over here instead of going
back with Skip," McQuaid suggested.

Riding quickly to the south, he headed directly into
the trees, for he was sure that was where Willy had
disappeared. In the trees, he paused to listen. He thought
he heard the sound of horses to the west toward Hatchet
Creek and he turned that way. As he came closer to the

creek, the sound became clearer and he knew he was on the right track.

The horses turned up Hatchet Canyon and McQuaid cautiously followed. He might be riding into a trap with Willy helping to spring it. Or he might be on a mission to save Willy. He had to assume that Willy was in danger.

There was no way out of Hatchet Canyon except the way they had come in. Whoever was ahead of McQuaid would have to make a stand when he caught up with them. It wasn't until Dan came in sight of the four horses in a break in the trees ahead that he was sure that they were not laying an ambush for him.

Three of the riders were concentrating on the fourth one, who was Willy.

The three dismounted and pulled Willy off his horse. McQuaid moved closer while the scuffle was going on but stopped when they all stood on the ground. He was within thirty yards of them now. He was sure the three were Walsh, Gideon, and Niccum, but the moon, out from behind the clouds now, was cut off by the foliage of the trees and he couldn't see too well.

"What have you told them?" That was Walsh.

"I haven't told anybody anything," Willy said.

"Do they know you're in this with us?" That was Gideon's voice.

"McQuaid guessed," Willy said. "But I ain't told nobody."

"He knows more than he ought to know." McQuaid was sure that was Niccum's voice.

"I didn't talk," Willy insisted.

"I believe him," Gideon said.

"I don't," Niccum snapped.

"Vinny's right," Walsh said. "He ain't any help to us. And if he decided to tell what he knows, we'd be in real trouble."

"I'll stay with you if that's what you want," Willy said, the fear in his voice almost a tangible thing.

"You sure ain't going back," Niccum said. "Especially if McQuaid has an idea you're with us. He'd make you talk."

"No, he wouldn't," Willy insisted.

"One way to make sure he don't," Walsh said.

"You've got it," Niccum agreed.

McQuaid knew what they meant. And they wouldn't wait to carry out the execution. If McQuaid started shooting, it would be three against one. But it was that or let them kill Willy. Willy could be a valuable asset to McQuaid and the Patzels. McQuaid was not one to let odds hamper him in his decisions. He dug the gun out of his holster.

XVI

The shadows were really too heavy under the trees for accurate shooting. But accuracy wasn't McQuaid's chief concern now. He wanted to disrupt the plans of those three gunmen.

His first shot was too high, but it had the effect of a bomb. All four men, including Willy, dived for cover. There was one difference. Walsh, Gideon, and Niccum dragged their horses with them into the trees. Willy didn't take time to get his horse.

McQuaid sent another shot after Walsh and Niccum. There was a great crashing around in the trees, and McQuaid guessed they were trying to get mounted. They must have thought they had been caught by several men. McQuaid fired twice more to reinforce that impression, then quickly reloaded his revolver.

Moving around through the trees to the spot where he'd seen Willy disappear, he halted and called softly. For a minute, there was no answer. Then Willy eased out from the shadow of a tree.

"Is that you, McQuaid?" he asked.

"Get your horse, Willy," McQuaid said. "Those jaspers are going to figure out mighty quick that there isn't a whole army after them and they'll come charging back down this canyon like a spring flood."

Willy ran over to his horse, which had shied away

only a few yards. With Willy mounted, McQuaid led the
way out of the canyon, following the trail along the creek.
There was no point in trying to keep their retreat quiet.
As soon as those three got over their initial scare, they'd
come looking for the man who had shot at them. And
they would be doubly eager to get rid of Willy now.

Once out of the canyon, McQuaid made a beeline for
the Hatchet Ranch, kicking his horse into a gallop, Willy
just a jump behind him. They were almost to the ranch
when three riders broke out of the trees far behind them.
They reined up there, then turned back into the trees.

Ollie Heinze met them at the corral. Willy was trem-
bling when he slid out of the saddle.

"Where did you find him?" Ollie asked.

"Up in Hatchet Canyon. Walsh, Gideon, and Niccum
had him. Looked like they intended to give him a lead
heart."

"Another minute and I'd have been dead," Willy said.

"I don't figure they'll give us any more trouble tonight," McQuaid said. "The Ustas weren't with them just
now."

"Won't hurt to keep an eye out till dawn, anyway,"
Ollie said.

Rocky came from the house. "I heard horses. What
happened?"

McQuaid turned to Willy. "Maybe you'd better tell
us all what was going on."

Willy nodded. They put the horses in the corral and
moved back to the bunkhouse.

"Ed Gideon and Toby Walsh mapped out a plan over
a month ago and Ed talked me into joining in with them,"
Willy said, finding the words difficult to get out.

"What kind of a plan?" Rocky asked impatiently.

"To take over all of Long Bow Valley," Willy said.

"I could kill them with my bare hands!" Rocky said,
breathing hard.

"Just hold onto your temper for one minute, will you?" McQuaid said. "I want to know a few more things about it. Why did you join up, Willy?"

"Because of the gold they said we'd get."

"Gold?" Ollie snorted. "What gold?"

"Walsh said there was gold up in Hatchet Canyon. They promised me a share if I'd go along with them. I didn't think then there'd be any real trouble for us. The Patzels and Ustas were already fighting. Walsh said as soon as they killed each other off, we'd take over."

Rocky had control of herself again now. "How did Toby Walsh know about the gold in the canyon?"

"I don't know where he found out. But he said Old Man Harris used to bring out nuggets so there had to be a real lode in there somewhere."

"Grandpa never found more than a few nuggets," Rocky said, "and nobody but his immediate family knew about that."

"It leaked out some way," Willy said.

"Has Walsh found any gold in there?" McQuaid asked.

"I don't think he's ever really looked. He figured that if we found the gold, either Frank Patzel or Cliff Usta would claim it. So we weren't going to look for the gold till the Patzels and Ustas were gone. Toby didn't think it would be hard to find in that small canyon."

"Walsh has helped the war along then?" McQuaid said.

"Sure. I think it was Walsh who shot Mr. Patzel. I found out their plan was to get both him and Cliff Usta. Then McQuaid showed up and that upset everything. Toby was sure McQuaid knew about the gold and would find it and get away before we got the land."

"If he thought it was that easy, why didn't he get it himself and then run?" Rocky asked.

"He thought about it after McQuaid came. But he couldn't do it with McQuaid right there. Besides, there might be a deep vein of it and he'd need more time."

"I suppose he still plans on getting the gold, doesn't he?"

"Sure he does. With Frank Patzel laid up and Cliff Usta dead, he thinks they can sweep everybody out of the valley in a day or two, then take over."

"He ain't got many brains," Ollie Heinze said. "Just running everybody out isn't going to give him the land. It'll still belong to the Ustas and Patzels."

Willy shook his head. "He didn't say anything about that. Maybe he thinks he can just claim it like Mr. Harris did and run everybody else out."

"Do you know anything about their plans to get rid of everybody?" McQuaid asked.

"Not much," Willy admitted. "I've been trying to get out of the whole deal ever since Toby shot Mr. Patzel. They did talk at the last meeting I had with them about kidnapping the two girls."

"Bonnie and me?" Rocky exploded.

Willy nodded. "They figured the two families would be glad to move out of the valley to save the girls' lives."

"That is absolutely crazy!" Rocky sputtered. "My folks would never give in to blackmail."

"I don't know," McQuaid said. "Parents will do almost anything for their kids." He turned to Willy. "Do you think they've given up that idea?"

"Probably," Willy said. "It was just an idea. They hadn't made any plans to do it."

"Where does Niccum fit in?" McQuaid asked. "He was up there tonight, wasn't he?"

Willy nodded. "Niccum is a good friend of Toby Walsh. Toby sent for him when it looked like we were going to need help."

"Looks to me like he's a gunfighter," McQuaid said.

"He is. Toby says he's even better than him. Niccum is to get a share, although I don't know how big. Toby was saying tonight he'd earned his share already. He was the one who killed Cliff Usta."

"I'm not surprised," McQuaid said. "How did he get to be a deputy sheriff?"

"I'm not sure, but I think Herb Ault's supposed to get a small cut of everything for giving Niccum that job and putting him up here at Arrow. Having Ault on their side keeps the law off them, too."

"With the law on their side, they just might manage to keep everybody else out of the valley while they prospect every inch of Hatchet Canyon," Ollie said.

Willy nodded. "They figure they have to get rid of you, McQuaid. Then they'll have it. They think they've got both ranches crippled."

"They haven't got rid of me yet," Rocky said sharply.

Ollie shook his head. "If McQuaid was gone, there'd only be me and Willy and Rocky here, and Kenny Coy and Skip Usta over there. Three men handy with guns could do about as they pleased."

"We're going over to Ustas tomorrow and get a truce," McQuaid said flatly. "If we join forces, we can put up a good scrap."

"I'm not joining up with the Ustas!" Rocky declared.

"I suppose you'd rather die alone than live with the Ustas?" McQuaid said angrily.

"We're fighting the Ustas, not loving them."

"You won't be doing either one if Walsh and his crowd kill you," McQuaid said sharply. "We're going to get a truce tomorrow."

Rocky glared at McQuaid for a minute. Then her face slowly fell. "Maybe you're right," she said, her voice dropping to a low pitch. "But you may have trouble convincing Skip and Aunt Jane."

"We'll give it a try," McQuaid said. "First thing tomorrow."

Rocky turned quickly and went back to the house. Ollie Heinze stared after her.

"Never thought I'd see the day when she'd give in on anything, especially to a man."

"She's not stupid," McQuaid said. "She can see that this is the only chance the Patzels and Ustas have."

"You can count on me from now on," Willy said. "I'm not the fighter that Ed and Toby are, but I'll do the best I can."

"Nobody can do better than that," McQuaid said.

There was very little night left. Ollie stayed on watch and McQuaid got a little sleep. After breakfast, he told Frank and Alice Patzel what he was proposing to do. Alice glared at him.

"We're not buddying up to the Ustas," she declared.

"Stand together or die alone," McQuaid said. "You can't whip that bunch by yourself."

"We can handle them with what we have right here."

McQuaid played his last card. "You won't have what you see here," he said. "If you're so bullheaded that you won't agree to a truce till you whip these outlaws, then I'm walking out."

Mrs. Patzel's eyes widened, then narrowed to slits. "And what if Jane and her bunch won't join up?"

"I'll stick with you, anyway, if you offer to join forces," McQuaid said. "I don't figure they're so blind they can't see what they're up against."

Alice Patzel gritted her teeth. "All right. Talk to them. But I know Jane. She won't budge."

"Maybe she will," Frank said from his bed in the corner. "Jane has lost all but Bonnie and her youngest son. She knows where she stands."

"I will not cross that creek!" Alice said emphatically.

"You won't have to," McQuaid said. "Rocky can do the talking."

"I'm no keener on this than Ma is," Rocky said. "But if we're going to do it, let's get it over with."

McQuaid nodded and headed for the corral. As they caught their horses, Ollie turned to Dan.

"How will we work it?"

"Rocky and you will come with me. Willy will stay here. He and Mrs. Patzel can handle anything that comes up till we get back. You and Rocky will wait at the creek. I'll go on under a white flag. If they'll talk, then you and Rocky can come on up."

"You're taking a big chance."

"I started this. I'll find out where it comes out."

"Why don't you do the bargaining, too?" Rocky asked.

"That will have to be done by a Patzel," McQuaid said. "If you can't face each other and agree to stop fighting, then no agreement I'd make would hold water."

Rocky sighed. "You're calling the cards."

Heinze shook his head in bewilderment as he finished saddling his horse. The three mounted and rode slowly toward the creek. If Walsh was there, he would likely shoot first and ask questions later. After all, the Ustas had made a raid on the Patzels last night. What could be more logical than for the Patzels to return the favor today?

They reached the river and reined up. So far there had been no warning shot from the other side. McQuaid was thinking that there wasn't likely to be a warning shot. With both Cliff and Morton Usta dead now, the remaining Usta crew was bound to be plenty jumpy. They'd probably shoot to kill.

Holding up a white piece of cloth in his right hand, McQuaid put his horse across the creek and rode slowly toward the Long Bow buildings. He was sure that someone must have seen him, but there was no sign of life as he rode into the yard and up to the door.

Dismounting, still holding the white cloth, he walked steadily toward the door. Just before he reached it, the door swung open. Skip Usta was there with a gun in his hand. But the gun wasn't pointed at McQuaid.

"What do you want?" he demanded.

"A truce," McQuaid said. "We're up against something that's going to take both outfits to handle."

Jane Usta suddenly appeared beside Skip. She had a gun in her hand, too, but it was aimed directly at McQuaid. The look on her face told him that she intended to use it.

XVII

"Hold it, Mrs. Usta!" McQuaid said sharply. "Listen to what I've got to say before you pull that trigger."

"You joined up with the Patzels," she said, wild eyes probing into him. "You ought to be shot."

"He says we're up against something that we can't lick alone, Ma," Skip said. "We'd better listen."

For the first time, Jane Usta took her eyes off McQuaid and looked at her son. "Why should we listen to the likes of him?"

"It's got something to do with Toby, hasn't it?" Skip asked McQuaid.

McQuaid nodded. "Toby Walsh and Ed Gideon are working together to drive everybody out of the valley."

"That don't change the fact that Cliff was killed last night," Jane Usta said. "And maybe by McQuaid himself."

McQuaid held up a hand. "Your husband was found behind the haystack, Mrs. Usta. Nobody at the Hatchet could have killed him there. He was shot in the back by that deputy sheriff, Niccum, according to what we learned. Niccum is in with Walsh and Gideon. They're trying to get rid of both you and the Patzels. They think they can drive everybody out now. They'll probably tackle one ranch at a time. If Sheriff Ault joins them, and it looks like he will, they'll have enough guns to handle either ranch alone."

Skip's eyes were shining. "You think if we join forces, we can whip them?"

"We'll have a chance, anyway. Alone, we won't."

"I don't believe Toby Walsh is double-crossing us," Jane Usta said.

"He is, Ma," Skip said. "Morton told me before he died that he caught Toby and Ed Gideon making plans. I checked the tracks where he was shot and Toby's boot prints were there. It was Toby who killed Morton, Ma. I know it."

"Pa said it was McQuaid," Mrs. Usta said.

"I tried to tell Pa what I knew but he wouldn't listen. Ma, we've got to join up with the Hatchet or we'll all be dead."

"I ain't stepping across that creek," Jane said. "If Alice wants to join forces, she'll have to come here."

"I'll go talk to them," Skip volunteered and stepped outside before his mother could object.

McQuaid turned toward the creek with Skip. Kenny Coy came out of the bunkhouse and joined them. McQuaid led his horse, not wanting to ride since the other two chose to walk the short distance.

"Before Morton died, he told Skip what he'd found out," McQuaid told Rocky and Ollie Heinze when they reached them. "Skip agrees we have to join forces."

"It ain't what I like," Skip said quickly. "But I figure we're all dead if we don't."

"Agreed," Ollie Heinze said. "Now we have to decide how to do it. What is Walsh liable to do first?"

"Get McQuaid if he can," Kenny Coy said without hesitation. "He's the top gun on either ranch."

"That's probably the key," Rocky said. "If Dan's out of it, they'll think they can handle the rest of us."

"Did Morton say anything about kidnapping Bonnie and Rocky?" McQuaid asked.

Skip shook his head. "Why would they do that?"

"They think the families would move out in exchange for getting the girls back safely."

Skip frowned. "I think Ma would do it to get Bonnie back. She's already lost Pa and Morton."

"My folks wouldn't do it," Rocky said. "They wouldn't knuckle under to save me or anybody else. Anyway, I don't intend to be kidnapped."

"I'll keep an eye on Bonnie," Skip said. "But how are we going to help each other if we're not together?"

"The ranches aren't far apart," McQuaid said. "If they tackle either place, the ones at the other ranch will come on the run to help out. That way we'll have the raiders caught between us."

"Sounds good," Kenny Coy agreed. "Won't take either one of us five minutes to get to the other place."

Coy and Skip Usta went back to the house while McQuaid, Rocky, and Ollie Heinze rode back to the Hatchet. It had worked out much better than McQuaid had hoped. But he still wondered if they had enough firepower to stand off all the guns that Walsh had.

"I think I'd better check things out," McQuaid said when they reached the ranch. "We'll have a much better chance of surviving if we know where they are and can figure out what they're planning to do."

McQuaid headed toward the upper end of the valley over Rocky's objections. But even Rocky could see that this was necessary, he thought. Surprise was the biggest weapon in a fight like this and the ranches were sitting ducks, having to wait until Walsh and his men decided to strike.

He rode cautiously, watching carefully for an ambush. Reaching Hatchet Creek without being challenged, he turned up the creek. The last he had seen of Walsh and the gunmen was near Hatchet Canyon after he'd taken Willy away from them. He guessed they would still be there, using the canyon as a headquarters. They might be searching the area for gold while they waited.

Before he reached the canyon mouth, he heard a horse behind him and pulled off the trail into the trees. He scowled as he saw Bonnie Usta coming up the trail. Reining out into the trail, he stopped her.

"What are you doing up here?" he demanded angrily. "Skip was to keep an eye on you."

"He tried," Bonnie said. "But I slipped away from him. I was in my room before and didn't know you were there till Skip told me. I saw you riding this way and decided I'd find out for myself what was going on."

"Skip surely told you that, too. Don't you believe your brother?"

"I do when he makes sense," Bonnie said. "But he said there was a plot to kidnap me. That doesn't make sense."

"It would if you'd just think about it," McQuaid said. "They kidnap you and Rocky, then tell your folks they'll kill you if they don't move out of the valley."

Bonnie's eyes grew wide. "They wouldn't really do that, would they?"

"I don't know. But we can't take the chance. So you get on back to the ranch and stay close to Skip. Don't go off alone again."

"Now you've got me scared," Bonnie said, shivering. "I'm afraid to ride home alone."

McQuaid wasn't sure whether she was really frightened or just saw a chance to coax him into riding with her. She loved attention from men, just the opposite of her cousin, Rocky.

"I'll ride part way with you," he volunteered. "Then you scoot on home and stay there till this is settled."

He rode down the trail with Bonnie to the mouth of Hatchet Creek. There she reined up. She obviously was no longer scared and wanted to talk. McQuaid wondered if she had taken a word he said seriously.

When McQuaid stopped his horse, he heard the sound of another horse coming from the east. He turned that way and saw Willy Lintz riding up the valley. He saw no reason for Willy's coming up here now, but he did see a chance to get on with the job he had started out to do. The longer he was out here, the better chance Walsh and his men had of laying an ambush for him if they had spotted him.

Willy rode almost directly to them, so McQuaid knew that he had seen them.

"What are you doing out here?" McQuaid demanded when the young puncher reined up.

"I saw Bonnie leave her ranch," Willy said. "I didn't know she was going to meet you. I knew the danger she was in and thought maybe I could head it off."

McQuaid nodded. "Why don't you ride back to the Long Bow with Bonnie? Then I can get on about my job."

Willy grinned. "Sounds good to me, if it's all right with her."

"Of course, it is," Bonnie said as sweet as a sun-ripened cherry.

Bonnie turned her horse across Long Bow Creek and Willy followed her. McQuaid chuckled as he saw how nervous and excited Willy was. Bonnie would have him eating out of her hand before they got to the Long Bow.

McQuaid turned back toward Hatchet Canyon. At the mouth, he stopped and searched as far as his eye could see. He couldn't see anybody, but he could see a dozen perfect spots for ambushes. If they were in there, they surely must have seen him as long as he'd been on Hatchet Creek. He'd be inviting disaster if he rode in there now. It wasn't worth the risk.

Reining around, he headed back to the Hatchet. Before he reached the yard, he saw the strange horse and rider there. Dropping his hand to his gun, he rode on until he saw Rocky standing a few feet in front of the stranger, a gun in her hand. The man on the horse was keeping his hands well from his sides.

He was smart, McQuaid thought as he nudged his horse on toward the yard. Some people might have challenged a girl's ability to hold a man at gunpoint. That would be a fatal mistake if Rocky was the girl.

Coming around the corrals where he could get a good look at the stranger, he relaxed. He hadn't expected Nick Joss to come out here until the fighting was over. He was a prospector turned gambler, not a fighter.

"Howdy, Nick," Dan said as he rode in.

"You know him?" Rocky demanded.

"He's from Central City," McQuaid said. "He's a dealer. Not a good one, maybe, but he makes a living off poorer hands with cards."

"He said he was a gambler," Rocky said. "But I didn't know whether to believe him or not."

"You played it right," McQuaid said. He turned to the gambler. "Why did you come up here now?"

"I got tired of waiting for any word from you," Joss said. "Appears I got here too soon."

"You're just in time if you want to do some fighting."

"If I wanted to fight, I'd have joined the army. Could you get her to put down that cannon?"

McQuaid grinned. "For a man in your business, you're not on very friendly terms with guns."

"Don't need to be if you play a square game."

"You still haven't told me what your connection is with him," Rocky said, still holding the gun on Joss.

"Sorry, Rocky," McQuaid said. "He found out I was coming up here to settle on that land on Hatchet Creek. He was a prospector before he turned to cards and he'd been in Hatchet Canyon. I promised to let him prospect in that canyon if I stayed on the land."

"You were getting mighty free with land that you didn't own," Rocky said testily.

"I wasn't sure then I'd stick it out," McQuaid said, "so the promise really didn't mean too much. He was to wait till the fighting was over before coming up here. Looks like he got impatient."

McQuaid could see that Rocky wasn't exactly thrilled with the idea of a stranger prospecting for gold in Hatchet Canyon.

"Since he's your friend, he can stay overnight," Rocky said, lowering the gun. "But he's not going to live up in that canyon."

"Glad I'm so welcome," Joss said, slowly putting his hands back on the saddle horn.

"You're lucky to get to stay at all," McQuaid said. "Get down and unsaddle your horse."

"How about looking at that canyon?" Joss asked.

"Go ahead if you want to get shot," McQuaid said. "I figure that's where the outlaws are holed up."

"I'll wait," Joss said quickly.

"You can make yourself useful if you'll help us in the fight," McQuaid said.

Joss shook his head. "All I stopped here for was to inquire where you were. I thought she was going to shoot me on general principles."

"Under the circumstances, I wouldn't have blamed her."

Willy came riding in from the Long Bow then, his eyes on the clouds. McQuaid spoke to him and he barely answered.

"She's the grandest girl alive," he said to nobody in particular.

McQuaid grinned at Ollie, who had come out in the yard. "He may not be worth much as a guard tonight," Dan said.

"He'd better be. They might strike any time."

The afternoon wore on toward evening with nothing to hint of trouble. Joss was impatient to get to Hatchet Canyon, but he balked at taking a turn at standing guard.

"If everything is quiet by morning, I'll take you up to Hatchet Canyon," McQuaid promised. "Might be dangerous, but you can have your look."

"Won't take me long to find out if there are any gold deposits there," Joss said. "Finding gold is worth taking the risk, I reckon."

"You're crazy, you know," McQuaid said. "We may have a battle royal before morning, anyway."

They divided into the same guard teams as the night before. But this time they kept close to the buildings. There would be no opportunity for another kidnapping.

The night passed quietly. McQuaid was surprised. The only explanation he could think of was that Walsh had some scheme in mind that would be better than open warfare. Walsh didn't strike McQuaid as a patient man. Something would have to break soon.

After breakfast McQuaid reluctantly took Nick Joss up the valley toward Hatchet Canyon. Rocky had asked how long McQuaid expected to be gone. He had promised to be back in an hour. If Joss wanted to stay, that would be his decision.

McQuaid used extreme caution as he rode into the canyon. But he saw nothing. That didn't put him at ease. If Walsh and his men weren't here, where were they? They hadn't given up their quest, not when they were this close to success.

"You start your prospecting," McQuaid told Joss. "I want to look around for signs of those gunmen."

Joss nodded and headed for the waterfall at the upper end of the canyon. McQuaid rode along the creek. If Walsh had camped in here, it had likely been near the creek.

Dan found the camp and dismounted. He touched the ashes; they were still warm. Breakfast had been cooked here, he guessed. If Walsh's bunch were not in the canyon now, they couldn't have been gone very long.

He searched the little canyon for another thirty min-

utes, finding no sign of them. They were gone. He realized he had already stayed here longer than he had told
Rocky he would. He should be back at the Hatchet now.
Walsh and his men might strike at any time, especially
if they knew he was gone.

Riding to the waterfall, McQuaid found Joss digging
away near the pool at the bottom of the falls.

"I'm going back to the ranch, Nick. Coming?"

Joss shook his head. "Found a couple of nuggets here.
I'm going to stay till I find where they came from. I'll
be down as soon as I do a little more work."

McQuaid rode back down the canyon and put his horse
to a lope. He suddenly felt trouble washing over him. He
wished he was back at the ranch right now.

Riding through the trees and out into the open, he
searched both ranches for signs of Walsh and his men.
He saw nothing. But he didn't relax. They hadn't come
out of the canyon for a joy ride.

Dan's horse was puffing when he rode into the yard
at the Hatchet. Willy and Ollie Heinze were both there.
He didn't see Rocky, but she was probably in the house.

"Seen anything of Walsh?" McQuaid asked before his
horse stopped.

Ollie shook his head. "What took you so long? Rocky
got worried and went out to look for you."

McQuaid hit the ground in front of Ollie. "You mean
she's gone?"

"She went through the trees. I went straight up the
creek. I just got back. She ain't back yet."

"Walsh and his men left the canyon this morning,"
McQuaid said. "I found their campfire. Still warm.
They're out here somewhere."

"Kidnapped!" Ollie said, the word choking in his
throat.

McQuaid nodded, just as sure of it as Ollie was.

XVIII

"Where'll we start looking for Rocky?" Willy asked.

Before McQuaid could give the question any thought, a horse splashed across the creek and galloped up toward the buildings. McQuaid recognized Kenny Coy, the foreman over at the Long Bow.

"Bonnie is gone," Coy panted as if he'd been doing the running instead of the horse.

"Where?" Ollie demanded.

"We don't know," Coy said. "She went out to feed the chickens. Didn't come back. We figure they got her."

"Thought you and Skip were going to watch her!" Willy yelled wildly.

"We didn't think she was in any danger feeding the chickens," Coy said. "They must have sneaked in like hungry coyotes."

"Looks that way," McQuaid said.

"I'm going after her right now!" Willy shouted.

"Take it easy, Willy," McQuaid said sharply. "You're no match for them even if you find them. We've got to get organized."

"They've got Bonnie," Willy wailed.

Coy looked from Willy to McQuaid. "He's got it bad, ain't he?"

McQuaid nodded. "Came home yesterday like that."

"That explains the way Bonnie was acting. She's far gone, too, I think."

161

"Rocky isn't here, either," McQuaid said. "Looks like they made good on their plan to kidnap the girls. Go back and bring Skip and his mother over here. We need to be together. They'll contact us if I don't miss my guess. They think this is going to be easier than fighting us all."

"I don't know whether I can get Mrs. Usta over here or not, but I'll try," Coy said.

Coy turned his horse and kicked him into a gallop toward the creek. Willy started for the corral to get his horse, but McQuaid stopped him. Ollie was almost as impatient as Willy.

"If we start out half-cocked, they'll pick us off like flies," McQuaid said. "Our only chance to get the girls back is to use our heads."

"You don't know those men," Willy said. "We can't leave the girls with them."

"I know their kind better than you do," McQuaid said grimly. "They'd like nothing better than for us to come charging out there looking for them. They'd shoot us down like ducks on a pond. Then they'd have the valley and the girls. I think they'll try to bargain with us for the girls' release. If we can't get the girls any other way, we'll go after them and hope we can rescue them alive."

McQuaid headed for the house to talk to Alice and Frank Patzel. Alice was livid with rage, but fear edged in to quiet her. Frank showed the worry in his face, too.

"We've got to do something right now," Alice said with determination.

"We have to wait," McQuaid argued. "They'll come around to see if you're willing to move out to get the girls free. They won't hurt the girls before that."

Frank sighed. "I reckon he's right, Alice. They wouldn't have any other reason for kidnapping the girls. We've got to wait."

Kenny Coy rode in a few minutes later, with Skip and Jane Usta in tow. McQuaid went out and helped take care of the horses. Jane Usta stayed outside and, even when the horses were in the corral and unsaddled, she balked at going inside. Finally Skip practically carried her into the Patzel kitchen.

McQuaid followed, wondering if the final battle of the war was going to be fought right here in this room. But Jane Usta refused to look at her sister, and Alice Patzel went into the other room where she couldn't see Jane. McQuaid knew now who the warlords were. It wasn't Frank Patzel and Cliff Usta who had kept this war going.

"I came over here to get somebody to go with me after Bonnie," Jane Usta announced. "No other reason."

"We'll get her back if we can," McQuaid promised.

"I'll go with anybody who'll go after Rocky," Alice called from the other room.

"What you two have to decide is what you're going to say when they make an offer to let the girls go if you'll move out of Long Bow Valley and stay out," McQuaid said.

"I won't give them an inch of Long Bow Valley," Alice said sharply.

"I'd rather see them dead," Jane snapped. "But I want Bonnie back."

"We'll wait a while longer," McQuaid said. "If they don't come here with an offer, we'll go out looking for them."

"Why wait?" Willy asked.

"In the first place, we don't know where they are," McQuaid explained. "In the second place, if we corner them before we rescue the girls, they'll kill the girls."

Seeing the impatience in all four of the men, McQuaid began making plans for tracking down the outlaws. But before he had finished, there was a yell out by the barn.

"That's one of them," Ollie said excitedly. "Let's pick him off."

"Hold on!" McQuaid snapped. "If you shoot him, they'll kill the girls. They've got the best hand now. We have to wait till we can see a way to outsmart them."

"Ain't no way but to kill them," Willy said.

"Do you want them to kill the girls?"

"If we can kill them from here, they won't have time to hurt the girls," Willy argued.

"Now you shut up and listen," McQuaid snapped, his patience at an end. "Walsh and those men with him are no fools. One of them has come here to do the talking. The others are holding the girls somewhere else. If we kill the man they sent to do the talking, those girls are as good as dead. Now do you want that?"

Willy scowled but said nothing. Ollie Heinze finally nodded in agreement with what McQuaid had said.

"What do you want out there?" McQuaid shouted.

"We've got a proposition to make. Who's in there?"

"We're all here," McQuaid said. "What's your proposition?"

"We've got Rocky and Bonnie. They won't be hurt if all the Long Bow and Hatchet outfits move out of the valley and never come back."

"Is that Walsh talking?" McQuaid asked quietly.

Coy nodded. "I'd know that voice anywhere."

"How are you going to know they'll stay out?" McQuaid shouted back.

There was a moment's hesitation. Then Walsh yelled again. "We'll take their word on that. But they won't get the girls till they pack up and leave."

"That'll take time," McQuaid said.

"We've got lots of time."

"We'll have to talk it over," McQuaid shouted.

"We can't let them have those girls that long," Jane Usta said.

McQuaid nodded. "Either you agree to leave and do it fast or we'll have to stall them till we think of something else to do."

"You don't think the girls are with them out there?" Willy asked.

McQuaid shook his head. "You can bet they're not.

Walsh is probably alone and Gideon and Niccum are back with the girls somewhere out of range of us." He sighed.

"Better think it over," McQuaid shouted to Walsh. "Even if everybody moves out, the land won't be yours."

"They're going to sign over the land they own," Walsh shouted back.

"Want to come in while we make up the papers?" McQuaid invited.

"You don't get me on that. We'll send in the papers and the Patzels and Ustas will sign them."

McQuaid heard another voice out there in the sudden silence. He turned to the others. "Who was that?"

Alice spoke up from the other room where she apparently was at a window. "That's Herb Ault. What's he doing with them?"

"Trying to get his paws on a share of the valley, too," Ollie said. "He probably brought the papers for Frank and Jane to sign. Being the sheriff, he could find out what land they owned and get the papers made up."

"That would mean that Niccum and Gideon are with the girls somewhere for sure," McQuaid said. He motioned the men closer. "I've got an idea. It may not work, but it's about the only chance we have."

"Anything's better than waiting," Ollie said.

"A couple of us will slip out the back way and try to get around the two at the barn. The other two somewhere back in the trees are probably with Rocky and Bonnie. We'll try to surprise them. There's a good chance we won't succeed, but I can't think of anything better."

"I'm for it," Willy said. "I'm going."

"I'll go after Bonnie," Coy said.

Skip put in his bid, too. McQuaid could see that Willy was going even if he had to disobey orders to do it.

"I'll decide who goes," McQuaid said. "I'm going, for one."

"I agree to that," Ollie said instantly. "Nobody has a

better chance of pulling it off than you. Who else?"

"Willy," McQuaid said. "He's got more at stake than almost anyone unless it's Bonnie's mother."

"I see what you mean," Coy said. "All right. What about the rest of us?"

"First, we've got to establish another spokesman," McQuaid said. "Then when we start out, you may have to begin shooting. If everybody handles a rifle, they'll never miss two of us."

"Who's going to do the talking to Walsh?" Ollie asked.

The answer came from the other room. "All right, you varmints!" Alice shouted. "McQuaid says I've got to do the dickering with you. It's Jane's and my girls you got."

McQuaid motioned to Willy and, without a word, they moved to the far side of the room. There was no cover behind the house. The only thing that worried McQuaid was that Niccum and Gideon might be someplace where they could watch the back of the house. If that was the way it was, then their plan would fail. It was a chance they had to take.

He heard Alice screaming at Walsh and he guessed that she had let her temper get the best of her and reason had gone out the window. The next instant a rifle roared from the other room.

Immediately a glass shattered in the kitchen as a rifle from the barn picked up the battle. McQuaid had thought all the windows had been broken the other night, but the first shot had found an unshattered one.

The rifles in the kitchen opened up then. Glancing back, McQuaid saw that Jane had picked up a rifle and was firing, too. With Ollie, Coy, and Skip joining in, that made five rifles. Walsh would never guess that two men had slipped out of the house.

"Watch the creek bank," McQuaid warned Willy softly. "They may be hiding there. If they're not, that's where we'll head. Keep the house between us and the barn."

McQuaid went through the window first. He dropped to the ground and rolled. But no shot came from the creek. Willy followed and still there were no shots. Niccum and Gideon must be up among the trees as McQuaid had first thought.

Bending low and keeping the house directly behind them, they ran to the creek and dropped over the bank. With a warning to follow him and keep low, McQuaid started up the creek. He wished now that trees lined Long Bow Creek the way they did Hatchet Creek. But it was good grass right down to the edge of the bank here.

McQuaid and Willy ran up the creek toward the trees that came down from Hatchet Creek. Behind them, McQuaid heard the rifles slow down and Alice's shrill voice took up the yelling again. Walsh yelled back.

"We're getting farther away," Willy complained.

"Can you see any faster way to get to those trees behind the barn?" McQuaid asked. "If you cut across where they can get even a glimpse of you, you'll be picked off and the girls are likely to be killed, too. Are you in that big a hurry?"

Willy scowled but said nothing. He kept his head down as they moved on to the trees that lined Hatchet Creek. The ranch house was quite a distance from them now, but McQuaid could still hear Alice's screams at Walsh and the rumble of his replies. Occasionally rifles roared. He had never taken part in a battle like that before. Either they talked or they fought. Here they were doing both.

McQuaid wasn't used to going so far on foot and he was puffing by the time they had gone up Hatchet Creek far enough to be able to turn back down the valley inside the trees.

"It will be next Christmas before we get to them," Willy panted.

"Maybe," McQuaid said, stopping to catch his breath. "We're not even sure where they are, either."

"How are we going to find them?"

"You go down through the trees close to the canyon wall. I'll go along this edge of the trees, making sure they don't see from the barn. If they're holding the girls back here in the trees, we ought to find them."

Willy nodded and started on the run through the trees.

McQuaid stopped him. "How do you figure on getting the girls free if you find them?"

Willy stopped and scowled. "I'll kill the men holding them," he said.

"And maybe kill the girls, too," McQuaid said. "Don't go off half-cocked. You were making as much noise as a herd of elephants. You've got to see them before they see you. Then maybe you'll get the chance to get the girls free without risking their lives."

Willy frowned but he nodded. Patience was not one of his virtues and this job was going to tax his patience to the limit. But McQuaid thought that his concern for Bonnie's safety would hold down his impetuosity.

As he moved quietly down through the trees, McQuaid kept one eye on the area ahead, hoping for sight of the men and the two girls. He looked frequently at the barn where the fighting continued. When he got even with the barn, he moved more cautiously. The girls should be around here somewhere if he had guessed right.

He saw the two men at the corners of the barn, firing at the house. He recognized Toby Walsh and the fat form of the sheriff, Herb Ault. There was no sign of anyone else there.

McQuaid turned all his attention then to the trees around him. He moved past the ranch buildings and was almost ready to give up his theory that the other members of Walsh's gang were holding the girls nearby when he caught a glimpse of color through the trees.

At the same time, he heard the rustle of a quiet struggle. Running silently forward, he came in sight of the combatants. He expected to see Willy involved. But it was Niccum and Rocky. Rocky had her hands tied behind her back, but that wasn't preventing her from fighting to get away from Niccum.

McQuaid moved closer, waiting for a break. He wouldn't have believed he could shoot a man without giving him some warning. But right now, he knew he could and he would if he got a clear shot at Niccum. The way he was manhandling Rocky made Dan's blood boil.

He had his gun in his hand as he ran forward. Niccum was partly turned away from him and his attention was concentrated on holding Rocky. Then suddenly Rocky jerked around and Niccum was spun around, too. He ended up facing McQuaid squarely. His face registered surprise which gave way almost instantly to hate. Grabbing Rocky tightly with one arm, he swung his gun on McQuaid.

XIX

McQuaid dived to one side, knowing he couldn't shoot. Niccum had Rocky almost in front of him as a shield.

Niccum's first shot went wild, but the second bullet found its mark. McQuaid felt the slap of the bullet in his leg. The next shot would surely finish him.

Jerking around where he could see Niccum, Dan also looked for the nearest tree, but it was ten feet away. Niccum wasn't shooting, however. Rocky had erupted into action, even though she was bound and held by one arm. She was powerful enough to force Niccum to use all his strength to hold her.

Still McQuaid could not get a clear shot. He wasn't sure he could have held his gun steady enough if he had.

Then Rocky got a foot free and swung a boot heel with all her strength back against Niccum's shin. He howled and for an instant loosened his grip on her. She dug an elbow into his stomach and threw herself forward. Frantically, he tried to hold her in front of him. But she hit the ground and rolled away.

McQuaid was having trouble holding his gun steady. Niccum fired quickly at McQuaid, then dived toward a tree. The bullet missed.

While Niccum was scrambling for protection, Mc-

Quaid lunged forward, finding he could maneuver some although that leg refused to respond to his demands. He got behind a tree himself and when Niccum peeked around the tree where he had taken refuge, McQuaid fired his first shot. It clipped bark from the tree an inch from Niccum's head.

Niccum dived back and McQuaid saw him dodging toward another tree farther away. He lunged for another tree himself. He couldn't let Niccum get away. He owed him something both for the way he'd been treating Rocky and for the bullet in his leg.

McQuaid fired every time he caught a glimpse of Niccum, and Niccum returned the fire, apparently taking time to reload as he dodged. Then, as Niccum was dodging from one tree to another, McQuaid hit him in the lower leg. Niccum went down, but he bounced up and dived behind a tree.

McQuaid knew he hadn't inflicted a serious wound, but it might hamper his escape. Dragging himself to another tree, he tried to see where Niccum had gone. Then Niccum moved from behind one tree and tried to make it to another, but his leg gave way.

Even as he fell, he wheeled to face McQuaid. McQuaid dragged himself out from behind his tree where he could get a clear shot at Niccum. Niccum came up to a stitting position and began firing. Two bullets snapped past McQuaid, while McQuaid brought up his gun, remembering not to hurry his shot. He fired only once. Niccum was bounced backward as if hit with a club. His gun dropped and he toppled over.

McQuaid limped forward slowly, dragging his wounded leg. Niccum's fight was over. Turning around, McQuaid looked back up the valley where he had last seen Rocky. He couldn't see her now, but she had to be up there.

Dragging his bad leg, he moved back to the spot where the fight had started. He was surprised how far away that was. He saw the blood on the ground where he had been hit. His pants leg was soaked with blood now. He'd have to get that wound taken care of.

But first he had to find Rocky. He heard shots farther down the valley but none over by the barn. He ignored the sounds of battle and began searching for Rocky. She should be close. Her legs had been free. Maybe she had run. But he couldn't believe she would have run away. She'd have run toward the fight.

Dan's leg was really hurting now, but he kept up his frantic search. Slowly the realization came to him that somebody must have caught Rocky again.

While McQuaid was studying the ground for any tracks that would verify his suspicions, Willy came running up from the valley. He had Bonnie with him.

"I got her," he shouted excitedly. "Did you get Rocky?"

"I thought I had," McQuaid said, leaning against a tree for support. "But she's not here now. Did Gideon have Bonnie?"

Willy nodded. "I beat him in a gunfight. Didn't think I could."

"Where is Rocky?" Bonnie asked.

"I figure somebody grabbed her again while I was fighting Niccum."

"You're hurt," Willy said, noticing the bloody leg. "How bad?"

"Bad enough," McQuaid said. "But I can't baby it now. Got to find Rocky."

"Look, coming from the barn," Bonnie said suddenly.

McQuaid turned that way. Herb Ault was waddling toward the trees as fast as he could come.

"Willy, you look for tracks to see where Rocky went. Walsh isn't with Ault, so he must have taken Rocky. I'm going to have a few words with the sheriff."

Willy started to object, then turned instead to search

the ground to the west, Bonnie going with him. McQuaid stationed himself behind some trees right in line with Ault's retreat. When the sheriff got to the trees, he heaved a sigh and paused to catch his breath.

McQuaid centered him with his gun. "Having fun shooting at people in that house, Ault?"

"Huh!" Ault lurched around, then froze when he saw McQuaid and the gun.

"Not a very good pastime for a sheriff," McQuaid said.

"Now wait a minute," Ault whimpered, his eyes on the gun. "I can tell you why I was there."

"I know why you were there," McQuaid said. "Where's Walsh?"

"Don't know," Ault growled. "He ran out on me, the coward."

"Since you think that it's such a good idea to drive everybody out of the valley with nothing, let's see you leave here the same way."

Ault visibly relaxed as he evidently concluded that McQuaid wasn't going to shoot him. "What does that mean?"

"Strip," McQuaid said. "Everything but your underwear. You're walking out without a horse or a gun or boots."

"You can't do that!" Ault howled.

"Try me and see," McQuaid said and cocked his gun.

Frantically, Ault began stripping off his clothes. When he was down to his underwear, McQuaid motioned with the gun.

"Get going. And if you get on your horse, I'll shoot you out of the saddle."

"I'll put you behind bars for this!" Ault yelled.

"Not after I tell the commissioners about the sheriff they appointed. I've got plenty of witnesses."

Ault, swearing both at McQuaid and the stickers that

punctured his feet with every step, started moving down the valley, keeping in the trees out of sight of the ranch buildings.

McQuaid watched Ault disappear in the trees. It had to have been Walsh who took Rocky. He'd use her as a hostage to escape from the valley. He doubted if Walsh had left the valley yet. He'd have had to come down past the spots where McQuaid was fighting Niccum and Willy was fighting with Gideon to get out of the valley. He had probably headed the other way.

Willy came back, leading two horses. They would be Niccum's and Gideon's. Walsh must have taken his own and Ault's for Rocky. Willy helped get McQuaid on one horse, put Bonnie on the other, and led them all down to the house in spite of McQuaid's objections. He wanted to go after Rocky.

Explanations were brief. Nobody at the house had been hurt. Jane, reunited with her daughter, ignored the rest of them. Alice quickly cleaned and dressed McQuaid's wound. The bullet had gone through. While it had torn a ragged hole and caused a lot of bleeding, it had made a clean wound. Rest was recommended, but McQuaid explained emphatically that there would be no rest for him till he found Rocky and Walsh.

No one opposed him. They all volunteered to go with him, but he selected only Ollie Heinze. Ollie was dependable and Rocky meant almost as much to him as a daughter would have.

Dan's leg felt a lot better as he hobbled out to his horse. Willy had him saddled and the rifle in its boot. Ollie got his horse and joined McQuaid. The day was almost gone. He wished it would last till he found Walsh and Rocky.

"Where do you figure we'll find him?" Ollie asked.

"Up the canyon," McQuaid said. "I'm sure he couldn't have gotten past us to go down. Probably figures on slipping out of the canyon during the night. It'll be dark in half an hour."

Ollie nodded and they rode out of the yard, heading up the valley. By then McQuaid knew his leg was going to give him trouble after all. He shouldn't be riding, but what he should or shouldn't be doing was of no consequence now. He was going to do what he had to do.

"Main valley or Hatchet Canyon?" Ollie asked when they hit Hatchet Creek.

"I'll go into Hatchet Canyon," McQuaid said. "You go on up the main valley. Make sure that he doesn't slip past you and get out."

Ollie nodded, looking up at the peaks that were tinted by the last glow of sunlight. "I told Willy and Skip and Kenny to spread out in the trees across the valley to make sure he didn't slip past there in case he got by us."

"Good," McQuaid said, gritting his teeth against the pain in his leg. "Let's see if we can flush Walsh out before dark. If he's up here, there's no way out except down past the ranches."

McQuaid nudged his horse into a walk up Hatchet Creek. He had to get away from Ollie before Ollie saw the pain his leg was causing him. He'd probably been foolish to insist on coming himself. But he didn't trust anyone else to handle Walsh. And he had to get to Rocky as soon as possible. He couldn't imagine sitting back at the house while someone else attempted to rescue her.

Riding through the mouth of Hatchet Canyon, Dan saw how quickly it was getting dark. Even quicker than he'd anticipated.

It was totally quiet in the canyon except for the noise his horse was making, picking its way over rocks and dead tree limbs. If Walsh was in here, he'd have plenty of warning that McQuaid was coming. As much as Dan hated to leave the saddle, he knew he had to do this on foot.

Gingerly dismounting, he tied his horse to a tree limb and proceeded up the canyon on foot. He walked with more than a limp, he almost dragged his right leg. He'd probably start the bleeding again, too. But if Walsh was in this canyon, he intended to find him.

He had moved about half the length of the canyon before he heard anything. He wasn't sure what the sound was. The moon was spilling its light into the canyon, but it was still dark under the trees. After listening for a minute and hearing nothing, McQuaid moved ahead cautiously. Then suddenly he heard two voices only a few yards ahead of him. Both were angry. He stopped, listening.

"Soon as the clouds cover that moon, we're getting out," Walsh growled.

"You'll never make it!" Rocky retorted. "You'll have to kill me to get me out of the valley!"

"Have it your own way," Walsh said. "I won't mind killing you. But not till we get past Arrow. You're my ticket out of here."

"McQuaid will never let you get out!"

"McQuaid is shot, remember?" Walsh said. "I saw him dragging a leg. He ain't going to rescue you. So get that out of your head."

"There are others," Rocky shouted. "Ollie and Willy. Somebody will stop you!"

Suddenly the sound of a struggle erupted up ahead. McQuaid limped forward. Finally he halted where he could see Walsh and Rocky at the edge of a small clearing. Rocky was putting up a gallant battle, but Walsh was too big for her.

"If that's the way you want it, you'll get it," he snarled. He dragged her by her bound hands to one of the horses. There he got his rope and then pulled her over to a tree. Quickly he wound the rope around her and the tree. "Now you can just stay there till it gets dark enough so we can make our way down the valley. Nobody'll see us then."

"You'll never make it," Rocky warned. "I'll make enough noise so everybody will hear me!"

"Oh, no, you won't! I'll lay a club along the side of your head. You won't come to till we're past Arrow."

Walsh stepped back to inspect his work with the rope. Satisfied, he turned back and, for the first time, moved out in the clearing away from Rocky and both horses.

McQuaid knew he'd never get a better chance. He drew his gun and stepped out from behind the tree at the edge of the clearing.

"Walsh!"

Walsh spun around, his hand darting to his gun, his eyes searching the shadows along the trees. McQuaid whipped up his gun.

Walsh saw him then and snapped a shot at him. The bullet slapped into a tree inches away from Dan's head. McQuaid was having trouble keeping his balance on his weakened leg, but he gritted his teeth and put his weight down on it, then held the gun steady. Walsh got off another shot that burned McQuaid's arm. But he didn't flinch. He squeezed the trigger twice in quick succession.

Walsh was driven back several feet, his gun firing once more into the air as he fell. Then he was down and the gun slid from his hand.

McQuaid limped forward, watching Walsh. But there was no need to watch him any longer. Walsh was dead. Dan turned to Rocky and quickly unwound the rope from the tree, then untied the rope holding her wrists together. It seemed the most natural thing in the world for her to put her arms around his neck and lay her head on his chest. He forgot the pain in his leg as he held her close.

"I knew you'd do it," she whispered.

"I thought you could do anything that a man can do," he said, half teasing, half challenging.

"I thought so, too—until you came along," she said,

lifting her head and looking him squarely in the eye. "You're a better man than I've ever seen before. And I don't intend to let you get away from me."

He grinned. "That sounds good to me, except for one thing. If we get married, young lady, I'm going to ask you, not the other way around."

"Whatever you say," she said and rested her head back against his chest.

McQuaid considered trying to get Walsh's body out of the canyon and decided it would be more than he could do to get it across the saddle of his horse. It would be all right till morning. He had to get Rocky back to the Hatchet and relieve the worry there.

McQuaid rode Walsh's horse back to the mouth of the canyon where he'd left his. Just as they reached it, Ollie came rushing up the creek.

"Heard the shots," he said. "What happened?"

"Walsh fought instead of giving up," McQuaid said. "Let's get Rocky back to the ranch."

It was like a celebration at the Hatchet when the three rode in. Rocky's concern, though, was for McQuaid's wound. It had started bleeding again. With the help of her mother, she dressed it, and McQuaid stretched out on the cot where they'd put him and dozed fitfully till morning.

The smell of frying eggs and bacon brought Dan to life although he didn't feel hungry. However, with Rocky sitting beside him, he ate what he could.

Breakfast was barely over when hoofbeats came charging in from the west. McQuaid wanted to see who it was, but his leg refused to hold him this morning. Willy went out and brought Nick Joss into the house.

"There's a dead man up there in the canyon," Joss panted as if he'd been running.

McQuaid explained about Walsh. "I forgot about you being up there."

"I was scared half to death with all that shooting," Joss said.

"Well, you'll have plenty of time now to look for your gold," McQuaid said.

"Don't need any more time for that," Joss said. "There ain't any gold deposit there. I found half a dozen little nuggets at the foot of the waterfall. But they had washed down from above. There's some claims back up in the hills where Hatchet Creek starts. I reckon that's where all the real gold is."

"If we'd have had a chance to look," Jane Usta said, "we'd have found it."

"It's not there, Ma," Bonnie said. "You heard what he said."

"We never could look because somebody was always busy fighting," Alice Patzel complained.

"You've been fighting over nothing," McQuaid said.

Alice stared at him, then at her sister. Jane Usta's jaw dropped.

"That was all we were fighting over," Jane said as if she couldn't believe it. "And there wasn't a thing there."

"Reckon that was what Walsh and Gideon were after, too," Ollie said. "All this killing for something that didn't exist."

"With nothing to fight about, maybe we can be family again," Bonnie suggested.

"I'm going to get out of the valley," Jane said. "With Cliff and Morton gone, there just isn't anything worth staying here for."

"I'm taking Frank to town, too," Alice Patzel said. "I can get a doctor there who might help him get back on his feet."

"Everybody wanted this valley," Ollie said. "Now nobody does."

"I still do," McQuaid put in. "At least, that little piece I filed on." He looked at Rocky beside him. "Are you willing to live up there?"

"Wherever you say," she said.

Eyebrows shot up all around the room. Finally, Frank Patzel spoke from the other room. "Looks like Rocky ain't going to leave with us, Alice. Maybe she could look after things here for us. Might be that she and McQuaid could live here on the Hatchet."

"We might for a while," Rocky said. "But that knoll up on Hatchet Creek is a good place to build a house."

"Can you use another hand?" Willy asked McQuaid. "I'd like to stay."

"We can look after Ma's Long Bow for her," Bonnie added.

"Figures," McQuaid said, grinning. "Looks like I'm going to need a lot of help."

"I'll get your forty head of cattle to you in a few days," Joss said as he turned toward the door.

"Hold on," McQuaid said. "You were giving me those cattle for the right to the gold in the canyon."

"Just the right to look for the gold," Joss corrected. "I looked and lost. Nick Joss pays his debts."

"Could I have a private word with my former partner?" McQuaid said to the others.

The room cleared in a minute, leaving Joss facing McQuaid.

"Going to try to make me go back and do some more digging?" Joss asked. "I thought you weren't interested in the gold."

"I just want to know if you're sure there isn't any there," McQuaid said. "You didn't have time to do much prospecting."

"If there's any there, it's farther down than I want to dig. I ain't saying it's not there, though. I just figured from what I heard that this fighting and killing here in the valley was over that gold. Since I ain't going to dig for it, I thought it might be better if everybody thought there wasn't any."

McQuaid grinned. "You're right." He held out his

hand. "I appreciate the way you played your cards."

Joss gripped his hand. "Sometime when you win a big pot, look me up."

Joss was gone then, most of the others following him into the yard. Rocky came back into the room with McQuaid.

"He didn't seem too disappointed in not finding gold," she said.

McQuaid shrugged. "He's a gambler. He knew he was taking a long shot."

She came close to his cot. "You told me you were going to hold that land on Hatchet Creek. I didn't think you could. Next time you tell me something, I'll believe it."

"You'd better believe it," McQuaid said, "especially when I tell you I'm going to hold onto the prettiest little spitfire in these mountains."

Her kiss told him she did believe that.